MONTANA MAVERICKS

Welcome to Big Sky Country, home of the Montana Mavericks! Where free-spirited men and women discover love on the range.

THE TRAIL TO TENACITY

Tenacity is the town that time forgot, home of down-to-earth cowboys who'd give you the (denim) shirt off their back. Through the toughest times, they've held their heads high, and they've never lost hope. Take a ride out this way and get to know the neighbors—you might even meet the maverick of your dreams!

Faith Hawkins had always liked to live dangerously. And what could be more dangerous than flirting with "just passing through" cowboy Caleb Strom? Caleb has made it clear he's not interested in a commitment, and that suits Faith just fine. Once burned, lesson learned, but neither of them counted on their chemistry or their common bonds. Both adopted. Both cautious. And, just possibly, meant to be!

Dear Reader,

Welcome back to Bronco, Montana, home of the famous Hawkins sisters. These rodeo stars have been falling in love recently, and now it's Faith's turn. After years spent traveling the rodeo circuit, she's considering settling down in Bronco to be near her family. That new lifestyle is enough of a change for her. She's not looking to add romance to the mix. But she's not opposed to having a good time with the right man.

Enter Caleb Strom. Although he is completely attracted to Faith, he's not interested in a romantic relationship. He is on a mission to find his birth father and can't even think of falling in love until that matter is settled.

Don't you love it when two people who are perfect for each other agree that they aren't interested in romance? Come along and watch as Faith and Caleb's friendship turns into love. Of course, there are a few bumps and bruises as they travel the road to their happily-ever-after, but that just adds to the fun.

I hope you enjoy reading *That Maverick of Mine* as much as I enjoyed writing it.

I love hearing from my readers. Drop me a line at kathydouglassbooks.com to let me know what you think about Faith and Caleb, and I promise to get back to you.

Happy Reading!

Kathy

THAT MAVERICK OF MINE

KATHY DOUGLASS

Special thanks and acknowledgment are given to
Kathy Douglass for her contribution to the
Montana Mavericks: The Trail to Tenacity miniseries.

PLEASE RECYCLE • THIS PRODUCT IS RECYCLABLE
Recycling programs for this product may not exist in your area.

ISBN-13: 978-1-335-14314-3

That Maverick of Mine

For questions and comments about the quality of this book, please contact us at CustomerService@Harlequin.com.

Harlequin Enterprises ULC
22 Adelaide St. West, 41st Floor
Toronto, Ontario M5H 4E3, Canada
www.Harlequin.com

Printed in Lithuania

Kathy Douglass is a lawyer turned author of sweet small-town contemporary romances. She is married to her very own hero and mother to two sons, who cheer her on as she tries to get her stubborn hero and heroine to realize they are meant to be together. She loves hearing from readers that something in her books made them laugh or cry. You can learn more about Kathy or contact her at kathydouglassbooks.com.

Books by Kathy Douglass

Montana Mavericks: The Trail to Tenacity

That Maverick of Mine

Montana Mavericks: The Anniversary Gift

Starting Over with the Maverick

Harlequin Special Edition

Montana Mavericks: Lassoing Love

Falling for Dr. Maverick

Aspen Creek Bachelors

Valentines for the Rancher
The Rancher's Baby
Wrangling a Family

Montana Mavericks: Brothers & Broncos

In the Ring with the Maverick

The Fortunes of Texas: The Wedding Gift

A Fortune in the Family

Visit the Author Profile page
at Harlequin.com for more titles.

This book is dedicated with love and appreciation to my husband and sons. Thank you for always supporting my dreams and encouraging me to follow them.

Chapter One

Caleb Strom stepped into the arena of the Bronco Convention Center and looked around. The arena, which held about four thousand seats, was packed with a raucous crowd who'd come to honor Brooks Langtree, one of rodeo's legendary cowboys. Thirty years ago, Langtree had won the Golden Buckle, a special tribute reserved for the profession's most promising new stars. From all accounts, he had gone on to have an illustrious career, winning numerous awards, being named Cowboy of the Year several times, and serving as a role model for another generation of rodeo riders. Now he was back in Bronco, Montana, and was being celebrated as part of the Golden Buckle Rodeo.

Caleb pulled the flyer announcing Brooks Langtree Day from his pocket and studied it again even though everything there was seared into his mind. He'd folded and unfolded the paper so many times that he'd worn creases in it. He remembered the first time he'd seen the announcement. He and some of his friends had been going to lunch at the diner back home in Tenacity, a town about one hundred miles away from Bronco. One of his buddies had picked up the flyer from a stack by the cash register and shared it with the others. They'd pointed out that Caleb and Brooks Langtree looked so much alike that the two of them could be related. The guys had teased him about hitting up his famous relative for a loan. Caleb had thought that his friends had been pulling his leg until he'd taken a glance at the flyer for himself. The face on the advertisement seemingly looking back at him had made him dizzy. The eyes, nose, chin and cheekbones were the same. Brooks Langtree looked like Caleb imagined he would in twenty years.

At first, Caleb tried to ignore the resemblance. What was that famous saying? Everyone has a twin somewhere in the world. The fact that his lookalike happened to be a famous rodeo rider twenty years his senior didn't mean that they were related. It could be pure coincidence. Physical resemblance wasn't proof. It didn't mean that Brooks Langtree was his long-lost biological father.

Even so, Caleb had begun investigating the other man. He'd gotten his hands on everything he could find. He'd found and devoured old interviews in rodeo magazines and newspaper articles. He'd watched a couple of short videos on YouTube. He'd studied the information so intently that he practically knew every word by heart. By all accounts, Brooks Langtree was honest and honorable. A man with a stellar character.

Not at all the kind of man who would abandon his own months-old infant. And certainly not the type to insist the child be given no information about him.

Iris and Nathan Strom had adopted Caleb as an infant. He couldn't have asked for better parents. They'd given him a wonderful childhood filled with love and joy. They had never hidden the fact that he had been adopted. It hadn't mattered to any of them. They were a real family.

The adoption had been closed and the Stroms knew next to nothing about Caleb's birth parents. In the past, he had been satisfied with the little that he'd known about them. His birth mother had died a few months after he'd been born, and his father had given him up for adoption shortly thereafter. It was only after he'd turned thirty that Caleb had begun to want to know more about where he'd come from.

Even so, the resemblance couldn't be ignored. Not only that, it was the only clue Caleb had to go on in his search to find his biological family. He hadn't been successful before now. Brooks Langtree was as good a place to resume the search as anywhere.

Was it possible that Brooks Langtree was the man Caleb was searching for?

Caleb refolded the paper and slipped it into his pocket, then gave his head a mental shake. He needed to slow down and stop jumping to conclusions. Caleb had come here in order to get a good look at the man in person. Given the size of the crowd, many of them already occupying the seats nearest the makeshift stage that had been erected in the middle of the arena, an up-close-and-personal look wasn't going to happen.

Caleb was so busy staring at the stage that he didn't notice the person in front of him had stopped walking until he bumped into her. The woman turned around and stared at him. An apology was forming on his lips as he looked into her face. Then every thought in his mind vanished except one. She was the most beautiful woman he had ever laid eyes on. He searched his mind for words to say, but he couldn't form a coherent sentence to save his life. The woman was staring at him with wide brown eyes. Wide, *beautiful* brown eyes. He noticed the expectant expression on her face a second before she shook her head in obvious disgust and turned away.

Caleb had never had trouble sweeping a woman off her feet, so being speechless and inept was a new experience for him. He could only attribute his clumsiness to being shook up at possibly seeing his birth father for the first time in thirty years.

As much as possibly seeing his birth father after all this time had him rattled, Caleb knew that was only a small part of the reason he was so flummoxed. The other was the stunning woman who was currently laughing and talking with several other women. One glance at her was all that it had taken to make his heart lurch. If he didn't want her to think that he was a total loser, he needed to do something fast. He knew it was impossible to make a second first impression, but hopefully, there was still time to improve on their initial interaction.

He tapped the woman on her shoulder. She spun around and stared at him, her right eyebrow raised. The expression on her face was a mixture of annoyance and curiosity. And it was totally sexy.

"I want to apologize for bumping into you earlier. I was a bit distracted and didn't watch where I was walking. I hope I didn't hurt you." He gave her his most charming smile—the one that generally had women eating out of his hand.

She stared at him for a long moment, and he held his breath as he awaited her response. Then she nodded and smiled. "I'm okay. I guess in a crowd this size a person should expect to be bumped into."

She started to turn back to the women with her and Caleb feared that he was about to lose the opportunity to get to know her better. He extended his hand and blurted, "I'm Caleb Strom."

Glancing over her shoulder, she smiled and then turned back to him. She took the hand he offered. "I'm Faith Hawkins."

"It's nice to meet you, Faith." Her hand was soft and warm and he was reluctant to release it. But he didn't want to look like a creep either by holding on too long, so he released her fingers. "Are you related to the Hawkins rodeo family?"

Faith nodded and smiled. "I am indeed."

"Your family is legendary." Caleb wasn't much of a rodeo fan, but he recognized the name from his rodeo research on Brooks Langtree. He'd seen a few references to the Hawkins women. Although he hadn't done more than skim the articles that mentioned their names, he knew that they—especially Hattie Hawkins, the matriarch of the family—had been influential in the sport.

"Some of us are. My grandmother was a trailblazer. My mother and aunts followed in her footsteps, making names for themselves as the Hawkins Sisters. The women of my generation are trying to live up to their illustrious reputations."

"From what I gather, you ladies are well on your way." Caleb smiled, grateful that he'd spent the time studying up on rodeo so he could be conversant.

"Thank you. We do our best."

He was searching for something to say to extend the

conversation when the crowd erupted in cheers and applause. Caleb had been so focused on Faith that he hadn't noticed that everyone else had settled into seats. Caleb's eyes darted around the stage, searching for Brooks Langtree. The older man was leaning against the side of his armchair, chatting with the woman seated beside him. Langtree said something that amused the woman and they both laughed. For a reason that escaped him, Caleb was irritated by the sight. He wasn't even sure if Brooks Langtree was his biological father, so the sight of him enjoying himself shouldn't be an annoyance. Not only that, it was ridiculous to expect the man not to have a good time on a day designed to celebrate his accomplishments.

Besides, Caleb surely didn't expect his biological father to be miserable after all this time. Thirty years had passed since Caleb had been given away. That was more than enough time for penance. By now, the man surely had come to grips with what he'd done and moved on with his life.

That is if Brooks Langtree actually was his father—something that had yet to be established. If all went according to plan, Caleb would discover the truth today. And if Brooks Langtree wasn't his biological father? Then Caleb wasn't any worse off than he'd been this morning. He'd simply spent an hour or so in the presence of a rodeo legend and his legion of fans. Not only that, he would have met a gorgeous woman.

Faith and the women sat down. Faith was in the aisle seat next to where Caleb was currently standing.

"Do you mind if I sit with you and your friends?" Caleb asked.

Faith nodded up at him and then spoke to the other women. As one, the others rose and scooted over a seat, leaving the aisle seat—next to Faith—vacant for Caleb. He couldn't have planned it better.

"Thank you," Caleb said, leaning over so he could whisper in Faith's ear. Her sweet scent filled his nostrils, wrapping around him and filling him with sudden desire so strong it shocked him.

"You're welcome," she whispered back. Her low, sultry voice suited her perfectly. With high cheekbones, full lips, dark brown eyes and clear brown skin, she was absolutely breathtaking. She was only about five foot two, but every inch of her was perfect. She looked delicate, but he knew she had to be strong in order to compete in rodeo like her family. He'd followed in his father's footsteps and was co-owner of Strom and Son Feed and Farm Supply, so he understood how important it was to carry on the family legacy.

Would he feel drawn to rodeo if he had been raised by Brooks Langtree? Would he be a bull rider or a bronc rider, competing in rodeos every week? Those questions couldn't be answered, even if it turned out that Brooks and Caleb were related. Greater minds than him had participated in the nature versus nurture debate.

Faith put her arm on the armrest between their seats, nudging his arm aside. When he looked at her, she flashed him a disarming smile. His heart skipped a beat in response. What was that about? This wasn't the first time an attractive woman had smiled at him. Not to be vain, but from the time he'd been a tyke, the opposite sex had been drawn to him. It wasn't something that he controlled. It just was.

Caleb couldn't allow Faith's grin to sweep him off his feet. Nor could he allow her armrest aggression to go unchallenged. As she'd done earlier, he raised a questioning eyebrow. When she acted as if she didn't get the message he knew he had to be more direct. "What are you doing?"

"This is my armrest. Yours is on the outside."

He looked around her. Her other arm was on the other armrest. "But you're using that one."

"Elizabeth doesn't care. Besides, you have the aisle seat. That is a bonus in and of itself."

"I didn't realize there was a rating system for arena seats."

She laughed, a sweet sound that sparked warmth inside his chest. "You don't expect me to believe that. Even little kids know the hierarchy."

"Let's pretend I don't know and you can enlighten me."

"It's fairly simple. Aisle seats are the best. The closer you get to the center, the worse the seats become. I had the ultimate seat, which I very generously gave to you, so naturally I get to use the armrest."

He didn't care about the armrest—or the aisle seat. He'd just wanted to sit beside her. But he was enjoying talking with her. "In that case, the armrest is yours."

"Thank you."

Geoff Burris, currently rodeo's biggest star and a resident of Bronco, approached the podium and Caleb and Faith turned their attention to the stage. Geoff welcomed everyone to the opening day of the Golden Buckle Rodeo and then began to talk about Brooks Langtree. The older man had quite an impressive biography. Not only had he been a huge star on the rodeo tour for years, he'd been a pioneer. He'd been the first Black cowboy to win the Golden Buckle.

As Geoff listed his numerous accomplishments—some of which Caleb had been unaware of—images of Brooks on horseback or riding bulls flashed on enormous screens around the arena. Watching the nearest screen, Caleb couldn't help but be impressed by the man's obvious skill.

"It is my honor to announce that today is Brooks Langtree Day," Geoff said, bringing his remarks to a close. "So please, let's give Brooks a Bronco welcome."

The crowd roared as Brooks Langtree rose from his seat and approached the podium. Geoff and Brooks embraced before the latter stepped up to the microphone.

Although Brooks Langtree was fifty years old, he had the muscular build of a much younger man. There didn't appear to be an ounce of fat on him. He was about six foot tall, with an erect bearing. Only a sprinkling of gray in his short-cropped black hair indicated his true age. A close-up of Langtree's face filled the screens and a shiver raced down Caleb's spine as he once more noticed the similarities to his own face. The pictures on the flyers hadn't lied.

Langtree's eyes sparkled with humor and his smile was friendly as he glanced around the arena, soaking in the applause.

When the cheers died down, Brooks spoke. "I'm honored to be here. It has been a very long time since I've been in Montana. Thank you so much for welcoming me back home."

The crowd erupted in applause again. Brooks was

clearly affected by the love the audience sent in his direction. He wiped a tear from his eye and then waved, starting at one side of the arena and turning slowly so that he included each corner in his greeting. Caleb's heart raced when Brooks turned to his section. He willed the other man to look directly at him, but Brooks didn't. Even if their eyes met, Caleb knew Brooks Langtree wouldn't know who he was. To him, Caleb would simply be another face in a sea of faces. A complete stranger.

Even if he was his biological father, Brooks Langtree hadn't raised Caleb. Nathan Strom had had that privilege. Nathan was Caleb's father in every way that mattered. Even so, the need to know where he had come from had grabbed on to Caleb and wouldn't release him no matter how desperately he struggled to get free. He wouldn't be at peace until he'd gotten answers from the man who had sired him and then walked away without a second glance.

Caleb sent those thoughts away and managed to keep them at bay as the ceremony continued. After other commendations, Hattie Hawkins, Faith's grandmother, approached the microphone. Caleb had expected her to add her praise of Langtree, so Caleb was surprised when she said, "Faith Hawkins, I need you to come to the stage."

Faith sighed, and Caleb turned to look at her. She'd buried her face in her hands and was shaking her head as she slid down in her seat. "I can't believe she did this."

"Go on," one of the women with her said.

"You know she isn't going to budge until you do," added another. "Unless she decides to come off that stage and drag you up there with her."

Hattie put a hand on her forehead and began to search

the crowd. Spotlights began moving around the audience. "I know you're out there somewhere. Don't be shy."

Caleb stood and stepped into the aisle. Instantly a spotlight landed on him and Faith.

"Thanks a lot, traitor," Faith muttered, looking at him. Although she was frowning, her eyes sparkled with mischief, assuring him that she didn't consider him a traitor after all.

"You're welcome," he said, flashing her a cheeky grin.

She stood and passed in front of him. Once more he inhaled a whiff of her sweet scent. Soft and slightly floral, it was enticing enough to get his imagination going in a manner totally inappropriate for the moment.

The spotlight followed Faith as she walked down the aisle and Caleb's eyes did the same. Her perfectly round bottom filled out her faded jeans and swayed with each step she took. She jogged up the stairs to the stage and stood beside her grandmother.

"You didn't think I was going to let this day pass unnoticed, did you?" Hattie asked. Although she was speaking to Faith, the microphone picked up her words so that the entire arena was privy to the conversation.

"I was hoping," Faith said, softly.

Hattie gestured to someone offstage. "Bring it out."

Two men wheeled a table holding an enormous, six-tiered cake onto the center of the stage. Two big numbers—a three and a zero—were in the middle of the top layer. Clearly Faith was thirty years old, the same age as he was.

"Since everyone is here, I thought we should celebrate your birthday with the entire town."

Faith shook her head. "But it's Brooks Langtree's day. I don't want to steal the spotlight from him."

"Nonsense," Brooks said. "There's plenty of attention to go around." He joined Hattie at the microphone and together they led the crowd in a rousing rendition of "Happy Birthday."

Faith stood there, looking uncomfortable, then relieved when the last strains of the song faded away. As she hugged her grandmother and shook Brooks's hand, several people began cutting the enormous cake and placing the slices on paper plates. They handed a few to Faith along with several paper napkins. Faith then returned to her seat and distributed the cake to the women with her. After she'd done that, she held two plates in her hands. She grinned and then offered one to Caleb.

"Thank you," he said, taking the cake from her. "You had me worried there for a minute."

"I had to make sure I had enough. As the saying goes, sisters before misters."

He laughed. "Is that right?"

"You'd better know it. But you wouldn't have been out of luck. There's cake enough for everyone."

The lights in the arena were turned up as people wearing shirts advertising the Golden Buckle Rodeo began passing out servings of cake to the audience.

"Maybe," Caleb said with a smile. "But somehow I think this piece will taste sweeter."

Faith sneaked glances at Caleb from the corner of her eyes. He had to be the best-looking man she'd ever seen. Surely he was in town specifically for today's event or new to town. If he lived in Bronco she would have noticed him before today. Men this attractive didn't generally fly under the radar for long. Even though she was certain she'd never seen him before today, there was something vaguely familiar about him. Try as she might, she couldn't put her finger on what. She had an excellent memory and never forgot a face or a name. If they'd met before, she would know. Still, she couldn't shake that feeling.

"Excuse me," a man distributing cake said, coming to stand behind Caleb.

"Sorry," Faith said, stepping out of the aisle and taking her seat. Caleb sat beside her and his shoulder brushed against her. Her skin heated and tingles raced down her spine. What was that about?

Caleb took a bite of cake. "Delicious. And by the way, happy birthday."

"Thanks." This wasn't the quiet celebration she'd had in mind, but she should have known her grandmother would do something like this. Hattie was nothing if not a showman. Decades removed from her groundbreaking rodeo career, Hattie Hawkins still knew how to command the spotlight. That ability to hold a crowd in the palm of her hand had been passed on to her daughters and granddaughters. Faith's cousin Audrey, rodeo's biggest star on the woman's circuit, had her wedding to Jack Burris as part of the Bronco Family Rodeo a couple of years ago. Faith didn't mind the attention—that was part of the job—but in her mind that was a bridge too far. Some parts of her life were too personal to share with her fans.

"How else are you going to celebrate? Besides having the world's biggest birthday party, that is," Caleb asked.

"This isn't my birthday party. Today is Brooks Langtree Day, remember? It just sort of got hijacked."

A strange expression crossed his face and vanished so quickly that Faith could have imagined it. "I got the impression that he didn't mind sharing the spotlight with you."

She shrugged.

"So," he said, when she only sat there, "what do you have planned for the rest of the day?"

"My sisters, cousins and I will be performing in the rodeo this afternoon."

"That sounds nice."

"Have you lived in Bronco long?" she asked, still trying to place him.

"I don't live here," he said, confirming her earlier thought.

"So you just came for this event?"

"Yes. I saw flyers announcing Brooks Langtree Day. I decided to come by and see if he lives up to the legend."

"Where do you live?" she asked. Faith didn't want this conversation to turn into an interrogation, but she was curious about Caleb. And more than a little attracted to him. She was still a relative newcomer to Bronco and he was the first man that she'd found remotely interesting. Not that she was looking to add a man to her life. A relationship was the furthest thing from her mind. She'd been burned enough times to last a lifetime and was more than a little gun-shy. But Caleb was interesting. And he didn't appear to be flirting with her. It was possible that they could become friends. A girl could never have too many friends.

"Tenacity."

She shook her head and grinned ruefully. "True confession. I haven't lived in Montana for long and I have no idea where that town is. Honestly, I've never heard of it."

"It's about an hour and a half away. It's not as upscale as Bronco, but it's home."

"If you're looking for a tour from a local, you've come to the right place," her sister Elizabeth said, leaning over Faith and talking to Caleb. "Faith is just the person to show you around. You might even stop and get a cuppa."

Faith kicked her sister's foot. Since they were each wearing boots, she knew Elizabeth didn't suffer a bit of pain. In fact, she only grinned.

"Cuppa?" Caleb asked.

"Elizabeth lived in Australia for years," Faith said. "Every once in a while she slips up and uses an Aussie term. She means coffee."

"I would love a tour from a local," Caleb said. "And I wouldn't say no to a cup of coffee."

"Like I said, I'm relatively new to Bronco."

"You've spent more time here than I have," Caleb said reasonably.

"True." Faith actually liked the idea of spending more time with him, so she didn't resist too much. "I'll tell you what. If you come by after the rodeo, I'll be glad to show you around."

"That sounds like a plan."

Caleb had finished his cake and he stood. The crowd had begun to disperse and he stepped into the aisle. "I need to get going. Ladies, thanks for letting me sit with you. I'll see you later, Faith."

Faith watched as he walked up the stairs, her eyes glued to his broad shoulders, trim waist and firm backside. His muscular physique was just one more thing to like about him. Not that she was counting.

Once Caleb had walked through the doors of the arena, Faith spun around to look at her sisters. "What is wrong with you guys?"

"What do you mean?" Tori asked, innocent as a baby.

"You know exactly what I mean. Why were you trying so hard to push us together? Foisting me on him like an unwanted Christmas fruitcake."

The others laughed. After a moment, Faith joined in.

"That man is gorgeous," Amy said.

"Consider putting the two of you together our birthday gift to you," Tori said with a wicked grin.

"I was looking forward to getting that pair of earrings I saw in Cimarron Rose," Faith said.

"If you don't want him, I'll take him off your hands," Elizabeth said.

"Like anyone would believe that. You're so in love with Jake that you can't see anyone but him," Faith said. Her sister had married Jake McCreery just a couple months ago, combining their respective children into a busy family of seven. "If Caleb had even looked in your direction, you would have run away so fast you'd set a new land speed record."

Elizabeth grinned. "True. But since there is nobody in your life right now, there is no reason why you can't hang around with Caleb."

"Exactly," Tori added. "He was nice and seems like he's a lot of fun."

"He is gorgeous," Faith admitted, agreeing with Amy's assessment. There was no sense pretending that she didn't find him attractive. That would be a blatant lie. He seemed to possess all of the qualities that she liked in a man. Funny. Kind. Considerate. At slightly over six feet, he was neither too tall nor too short. He was muscular, but not overly so. He still had a neck. She absolutely loathed those guys who looked like they swallowed steroids daily and somehow ended up with no neck.

She also liked the way he dressed. His jeans were casual and his polo wasn't too tight or too loose. Like Goldilocks said, he was just right. And given her decision not to become involved with anyone, he was completely wrong.

But then, she'd always liked to live dangerously. Besides, what was the harm in a little fun?

Chapter Two

Faith brushed her horse one last time before handing her reins over to Glenn, the stable employee who led Sugarcane into the trailer. Although she loved her horse, the house she rented in Bronco didn't have the acreage a horse needed to be happy. So, like her sisters, cousins and their numerous in-laws who competed in rodeo, she boarded her horse at one of the local stables. Faith had confidence in the owner and the employees who cared for Sugarcane, but she went to the stables each day to care for her horse and to practice her skills.

Once Glenn drove away from the convention center, Faith went to the locker room where her sisters and cousins were gathering up their belongings. Today's event had been an exhibition as opposed to a competition with ranking points, but they had done their best to put on a good show. It was never a good idea to slack off at any time. Bad habits were easy to develop but hard to shake off.

"Good show," Audrey, Faith's cousin said, giving her a hug. Audrey worked hard to maintain her status as the undisputed champion on the women's circuit.

"Thanks. But you'd better watch out. I'm coming for your crown."

Audrey laughed and winked. "It's good to have a goal."

"So I've been told."

"Happy birthday, by the way. Let's get together for lunch one day next week. My treat."

"Sounds good."

"Elizabeth wanted me to tell you that she spotted your birthday gift in the audience. She said you would know what that means."

Faith waved off the comment. "You know my sister's sense of humor."

"I do. And I also know your ability to change the subject. That could only mean one thing. This gift is a man."

Faith knew it would be futile to deny it. She and her cousins had grown up together. They'd spent so much time with each other that they were as close as sisters. There was no fooling each other. "Yes."

"This man wouldn't by chance be Truett McCoy?"

"Tru McCoy? The Hollywood actor? Are you kidding me?"

Audrey nodded. "Jack told me that he might be here today."

"Why would a big star be in Bronco of all places?"

"I figure since he stars in cowboy movies he might want an up-close-and-personal view."

Faith only shook her head. Audrey's husband, Jack Burris, and his brother Geoff were famous both inside and outside of rodeo circles and they might hobnob with celebrities, but Faith didn't. "No such luck. We met a guy this afternoon. He sat with us during Brooks Langtree's presentation. Before I knew what was happening, Elizabeth had volunteered me to show him around town."

"How do you feel about that? If you don't want to be

bothered, I can have Jack and his brothers get rid of him for you." Audrey grinned. "I didn't mean that as sinister as it sounded."

"Actually I don't mind. He seemed like a good guy." Yet there was something about him that was a bit off. Not that she thought he was up to no good. She could read trouble from a mile off. Her sisters had equally good Spidey senses too, so one of them would have known if Caleb wasn't a good guy. He just seemed to be a bit distracted, which, considering he'd driven over an hour just to attend the ceremony, was a bit odd. But there was no crime in being distracted. She'd found her own attention straying to Caleb once or twice this afternoon.

"Well, then, let your hair down and go enjoy your birthday present." Audrey flashed a mischievous smile, shimmied her shoulders and then walked away.

Shaking her head at her cousin's antics, Faith changed out of her rodeo garb and into her most flattering pair of jeans and a new top that she'd gotten the other day at Cimarron Rose, her favorite Bronco boutique. She freed her hair from the scrunchie that held it away from her face, ran a comb through her hair, touched up her lipstick, then went to meet Caleb.

As she headed into the arena, her heart began to pound and her tingles skipped down her spine. *Don't be ridiculous. This isn't a date and Caleb isn't a potential love interest.* They were simply going to spend an hour or so together while she showed him around Bronco. If things went well, they might grab a drink at Bronco Java and Juice. If things went *very* well, she might suggest they grab a burger. If not, they'd go back to their cars, say good-night and go their respective ways.

Caleb was sitting in the front row when she entered, his long legs stretched in front of him. There were a few stragglers lingering at the back of the arena as if unwilling for the night to end. A number of workers were raking the dirt floor, getting it in shape for tomorrow's events. It was so quiet now that it was hard to believe that thousands of cheering people had been in here only thirty minutes ago.

When Caleb noticed her, he stood and walked over. He smiled and Faith instantly felt comfortable. There was something about him that put her at ease. Suddenly she couldn't wait to get the night started.

"That was some spectacular riding you did," Caleb said by way of greeting. "You're a great barrel racer."

Warmth flooded her and she smiled. "Thanks. Sugarcane and I have been working together for years. She knows when and how I want to move, which saves valuable seconds."

"You're a great team."

"Thank you again." She looked at him. "What would you like to see first?"

"I wasn't kidding earlier when I said that I didn't know anything about Bronco. I don't know what to ask to see. Perhaps a better question would be what do you want to show me?"

"That depends on whether you want to see Bronco Heights or Bronco Valley."

"I didn't know there were two Broncos."

"I'm still learning the difference, so take what I say with a grain of salt."

"Where did you live before, if you don't mind my asking."

"South America. I traveled the rodeo circuit there for a while. My cousins actually settled in Bronco first. Then more of my family followed. I guess the Hawkins family is gradually taking over."

He laughed. "A stealth invasion."

She laughed with him. "In a manner of speaking."

They talked easily as they walked side by side to the parking lot. Her Escape was parked near the entrance of the arena. A late-model pickup truck was parked a few rows away. The Bronco Convention Center was on the outskirts of town, so in order to get to any of the places Faith wanted to show him, they would need to drive.

"I know you don't know me well," Caleb said, "so if you would feel more comfortable, I can always follow you to town."

Faith smiled. She may have just met him, but she knew she was in no danger from him. At least not physically. She wasn't as sure about her heart. There was something about him that appealed to her on an elemental level. But since she wasn't going to open herself up for a romance, her attraction was immaterial. "I feel perfectly safe with you. But we are a ways from town. It makes more sense for each of us to drive there, so we won't have to double back later."

He seemed disappointed, but he nodded. "I'll follow you."

"Which side of Bronco would you like to see?"

"You were going to explain the difference to me." He shifted his Stetson away from his forehead and lifted one side of his mouth in a half smile. The expression was so sexy that her heart skipped a beat. She ordered her body to knock it off.

"Bronco Heights is where the rich folk live. Big houses. Big lots. All that. Bronco Valley is where the middle-class people like myself and my family live. Older homes and smaller lots. For the most part, everyone gets along well. Friendships aren't based upon class or anything like that."

He nodded, so she continued.

"Each place has its own downtown area with its own restaurants and stores. People from Bronco Valley go to Bronco Heights and vice versa. It just depends on what you are looking for. So, Caleb, what are you looking for?"

He shrugged his massive shoulders and her mouth went dry. She reminded herself that tonight was a one-time thing. She wasn't in the market for a man. "Just take me to your favorite places."

"I can do that."

Once they were in their cars, Faith led the way to town. Traffic was light and before long she'd reached Bronco Valley. She pulled onto a side street with plenty of parking spots, got out of her car and waited while Caleb parked his pickup.

"This looks nice," Caleb said once he was beside her.

"I enjoy walking around Bronco. There are so many interesting shops and good restaurants. Even though I haven't lived here long it already feels like home."

"Where did you grow up?" Caleb asked as they walked down the street. There were a few other pedestrians taking advantage of the beautiful fall evening, but the pavement wasn't crowded.

"Everywhere. My mother and her sisters were also on the rodeo tour and my sisters, cousins and I traveled with them."

"What was that like?"

She paused as she gave his question some thought. "There were things I enjoyed. I liked seeing different places and meeting new people. The adventure of it all. It's a big world and I want to see as much of it as possible. But there were times when I wished we didn't travel as much. Times when I wanted to live in one place for years instead of just a short time. But even as a child, I knew that it wasn't possible to do both things at the same time. Choices had to be made."

"Are you planning on settling down in Bronco or will you be moving along?"

"That's a good question. I do like Bronco. Some of my family members have begun to put down roots. They've either married local men or are involved in serious relationships. My parents came to town for my sister's wedding and they decided to stay for a while. I like being around my family and having a home base. As long as I'm competing on the rodeo circuit, I'll be able to satisfy my wanderlust."

"So you have the best of both worlds. It can't get much better than that."

"No, it couldn't." Of course, having a special someone to share that world would be nice. Not that she would say that out loud. She didn't want Caleb to think that she wanted him to fill that role. To be honest, she wasn't sure she wanted anyone to fill that spot in her life. She'd tried getting serious once before and the relationship had been an unmitigated disaster. Besides, she was enjoying the single life. There was plenty of time to fall in love in the future.

"This place looks interesting," Caleb said, stopping in front of Cimarron Rose boutique.

"It's one of my favorite stores. They sell the most beautiful boho chic clothing and jewelry. Some of it is a bit pricey, but it's all exquisite."

"I don't know boho chic from regular chic, but the stuff in the window looks nice. I could find some nice gifts here."

For whom? Did he have a girlfriend? It suddenly occurred to Faith how little she knew about Caleb. "If you're looking for something special for that certain someone, this is the place to go. Of course, if you're looking for high-end jewelry, I'd suggest Beaumont and Rossi's Fine Jewels."

Caleb gave her an odd look and she knew her fishing expedition had been very obvious. "I was thinking about my mother. She loves antique jewelry."

"Oh. Okay."

He looked her straight in the eyes. "And just for the record, there is no *certain someone* in my life."

Caleb's voice rang with sincerity and his eyes were clear and honest. Faith had no doubt that he was telling her the truth, and she appreciated his truthfulness. "Even though you haven't asked, there is nobody special in my life either. To be honest, I'm not looking."

"I sense a story there."

She shrugged. "It's not an original one nor one worthy of sharing. Suffice it to say that the last guy I dated was seeing me and someone else at the same time. He didn't tell either of us. When I found out, it hurt."

"Were you in love with him?"

"Not even a little bit. My heart wasn't broken. It was the fact that he lied to me that disappointed me. I don't think anyone should stay in a relationship that they don't want to be in. Not everyone is made for commitment or monogamy. But I do think that people should be honest about what they want. If they no longer want to be in an exclusive relationship, they should let the other person know. Deception hurts."

He nodded. "I agree. For the record, I'm not looking for a special someone either. And now that we've established that we're on the same page when it comes to relationships, can we go inside and look around?"

"Sure."

Caleb held the door for Faith before following her inside. There were only a couple of other shoppers, so they were free to walk about at their leisure. Faith loved it here. All of the items might not be her style, but they were all elegant in their own ways.

"What do you think?" Caleb asked, holding up a pair of silver chandelier earrings.

"I like them. They go so well with your skin tone."

"You think?" Caleb asked, not the least bit fazed. "Maybe I should get the gold."

She laughed. His sense of humor matched hers.

"Nah. Stick with silver."

"I think my mom would love these."

"She has good taste. They're beautiful."

They looked around a bit more, checking out other pieces of jewelry. In the end, Caleb decided to stick with the pair that he'd picked out initially. He paid for the jewelry and they continued their tour of the town, stopping in random businesses on occasion. Eventually they came upon Bronco Burgers.

"Would you like to get something to eat?" Caleb asked.

"Yes. I can't tell you how hungry I am. I'm always starving after I ride."

"Why didn't you say something earlier?"

She shrugged. "We agreed that I would show you around town, not that we would go out to dinner."

"Faith." The way he said her name spoke volumes. It also sent shivers racing down her spine. "That didn't mean that we couldn't grab a bite."

"I think I knew that."

"Do you want to get a burger here or would you rather go somewhere else to eat?"

"I would love a burger," Faith said. "I've eaten here a couple of times before. They have the best shakes."

"Sounds perfect."

The minute they stepped inside, the wonderful aroma of grilled beef surrounded them. Faith's stomach rumbled. "Sorry."

"Don't worry about it."

They grabbed seats and then placed their orders.

"I've told you a bit about Bronco. Can you tell me about Tenacity?"

"Sure. The name suits the town. People there are strong with a never-say-die attitude. Tenacity is a blue-collar town made up of ranchers."

"Are you and your parents ranchers?"

"No. We actually own a store. Strom and Son Feed and Farm Supply. I know that's a mouthful. We serve the ranchers in Tenacity as well as those in the vicinity."

Faith gave him a long, searching look. "I can totally see you doing that. You have a calm demeanor and a way of putting people at ease. More than that, you're honest yet diplomatic. You probably get a lot of repeat business because of that."

He seemed flustered. "I don't know whether you're pulling my leg or not."

"Not at all. I'm being completely honest."

He exhaled. "We do get a lot of repeat business. But that has more to do with my father than it does with me. My father only gets the best supplies so customers never have to worry about quality. He anticipates what people will need and stocks it ahead of time. If someone makes a special request, he does his best to fill it in a timely manner."

"That's good business."

The waitress brought their meals and they didn't speak until she had walked away. Faith took a big bite of her burger and then sighed. Delicious.

Caleb bit into his too, and his eyes closed briefly. "This is really good."

"It's the perfect after-rodeo meal."

"I know that Bronco has a couple of other rodeos. One at Christmas and one in the summer. Did you compete in those?"

"The one in December is the Mistletoe Rodeo. The other is the Bronco Summer Family Rodeo. And no, I didn't participate in either of them. My sisters Tori, Amy and I were touring in South America last year. I only moved to Bronco recently and was still getting a lay of the land this past summer."

"This must be a big change."

"In some ways. But rodeo is rodeo. Same events. Same scoring system. Same smells. And rodeo people are the same all over the world. Close-knit and caring.

Supportive. We compete against each other in the ring, but once the event ends, we're friends. Family, really. We all try to do our best, but we're happy for whoever wins."

"Why did you decide to come back to the States?"

"It was time. Don't get me wrong, I enjoyed being in South America. I saw a lot of tourist sights and had a lot of experiences I wouldn't have had otherwise. But my family seemed to be gathering in Bronco. My sister Elizabeth was actually touring in Australia before she came here. She was widowed a few years ago and has five-year-old twin daughters. Now she's married to a local rancher with three kids."

"Wow. That's a lot of kids."

"Elizabeth has a big heart and plenty of love for all of them."

"That's good. Kids deserve love."

"Speaking of kids. Do you have any brothers or sisters?"

He hesitated ever so slightly as if unsure how to answer. "No. I'm an only child."

"What was that like?"

"Good. I have great parents."

"Did you ever feel lonely?"

"Of course. Didn't you?"

She started to say that with four sisters and numerous cousins someone was always around, but that simply meant that she was seldom alone. Their presence didn't keep her from experiencing occasional bouts of loneliness. "Yes. I guess I did."

"I don't think the presence or absence of others keeps us from experiencing the whole range of emotions. We can try to use others to avoid feelings we don't want to acknowledge, but they're always there, lurking in the background until you deal with them."

"Impressive." She looked into his intelligent eyes. "What are you, a psychologist or a business owner?"

"I'm just a man."

A man she was beginning to like. Although she wasn't looking for a relationship, she now realized that by avoiding men altogether, she'd given her most recent ex-boyfriend control of her future. Since she hadn't been willing to give him a say over her life in the past, why would she give him that power now?

"How long are you going to be in Bronco?" Faith asked.

"I'll be going back to Tenacity Monday morning. I have a few things to take care of this weekend."

His words were vague, and Faith waited, expecting him to clarify them or give more details. Rather than do that, he picked up his cup and drained his strawberry shake. She shoved down her curiosity. They were little more than strangers. She wasn't entitled to know his itinerary. Nor did he owe her an explanation. Even so, they had talked so easily tonight it was disappointing for him to clam up now. Her Spidey senses went off but she told herself she was overreacting. His behavior didn't warrant her suspicion.

The waitress brought their bill and Faith reached for her purse.

"I have it," Caleb said, pulling his wallet from his pocket.

"That's not necessary."

"It *is* necessary. I enjoyed the pleasure of your company."

"I enjoyed your company, too," she said.

"Then consider this my birthday present to you."

Before Faith could argue further, Caleb handed the waitress several bills. "Keep the change."

The waitress looked at the money and then flashed Caleb a wide smile. "Thank you. Have a wonderful evening. Both of you."

Caleb nodded, then he and Faith left the restaurant. The October evening was pleasant and the air was crisp. As they walked down the street, dried leaves crunched under their boots. Faith glanced up at Caleb. "I love this time of year."

"Do you?"

"Yes. It's not too hot and it's not too cold. After a long, hot summer, it's nice to have cooler weather. And I'm a pumpkin spice kinda girl, so that's also nice."

"I have no idea what that means."

Laughing, she shook her head. "Pumpkin spice is a flavor. It's hard if not impossible to find in the spring and summer. But come autumn, it's everywhere. There are pumpkin spice lattes, cookies, biscuits, and even cereal to name a few things."

Caleb made a face.

"I take it you aren't a fan."

"It doesn't sound like something I would like, but I'm not going to say no without even trying it."

"If you like coffee, there is pumpkin spice creamer. That's my favorite."

"I prefer my coffee black."

"You aren't going to make this easy, are you?"

He chuckled. It was a happy sound that sent butterflies loose in her stomach. "Where would the fun be in that?"

"Fine. You like cookies, don't you?"

"I wouldn't say no to an oatmeal raisin or sugar cookie."

"Good. As soon as it's available, I'm getting some pumpkin spice sugar cookie dough. I'm going to bake a batch of cookies and you're going to love every bite. In fact, you're going to beg me to make you some more."

"You must be pretty confident in those cookies."

"I am actually underselling them."

"I have an excellent memory, so I'm not going to forget this brag."

"I don't want you to. I want you to remember every word that I've said."

He gave her a sexy smile that made her toes tingle. "I'm going to remember everything about tonight."

So would she.

They talked and laughed as they walked for another block before turning and going back the way they'd come. When they reached her car, he leaned against the hood. She leaned beside him. A breeze blew and his scent wafted around her. His cologne was slightly woodsy and totally enticing. Her knees wobbled. If she hadn't been propped against the car, she might have slid onto the ground.

While they'd been strolling around town, the sun had set and the moon had risen in the deep blue sky. Stars were beginning to pop out all over. Suddenly everything around them felt romantic.

Faith turned to face him. "I had a great time tonight, Caleb."

"So did I. Thank you for taking the time to show me around." His voice was deep. Husky.

"You're welcome."

They stood there for a moment, staring into each

other's eyes, not talking. Words weren't necessary as they basked in the pleasure of each other's company. She could happily stay here all night, but she needed to get home. She sighed. "I suppose it's time to say good-night."

"I know." He pushed away from the car and held out his hand. When she took it, he led her around the car to the driver's door. She fumbled through her purse until she found her car keys. She pressed the key fob, disengaging the lock. Caleb opened the door and held it while she slid inside. He waited until she'd fastened the seat belt before speaking.

"Would you mind texting me to let me know you made it home safe?"

"I don't mind, Caleb." Touched by his concern, Faith couldn't make her voice rise above a whisper.

They quickly exchanged numbers. Then Caleb closed her car door. Faith watched as he ambled over to his truck and hopped inside.

When Caleb was out of sight, Faith blew out a breath, turned the key in the ignition and drove away. As she went down the street, one thought played through her mind.

She really wanted to see Caleb again.

Chapter Three

Caleb drove the short distance to the Bronco Bed and Breakfast where he was staying the weekend. The B and B was in a six-bedroom, yellow Victorian house. The owner, Claire, a single woman in her midthirties, explained that she'd recently inherited the house from a long-lost uncle and had converted it into this B and B. She was friendly and respected her guests' privacy, something that given his situation, he appreciated.

His second-floor room was small yet cozy and the blue-and-cream color scheme was relaxing. The queen bed was comfortable and there was an old-fashioned rolltop desk where he'd set up his laptop. Stepping out of his boots, he settled into the armchair in front of the window and propped his feet on the footstool. He needed to update his parents. When he'd told his parents of his plans to find his birth father, they hadn't been surprised. It was as if they'd always known the day would come.

The funny thing was, until he'd turned thirty, he hadn't given the idea much thought. Sure, he'd occasionally wondered about his birth parents, but the notion had always been fleeting. This time had been different. Once the idea had entered his mind, he couldn't shake it. He still didn't understand why. His parents were the best and he'd grown up surrounded by their unconditional love. They'd never once treated him as anything other than their precious son.

So why was the need to find his biological parent so strong?

When he'd decided to go in search of his past, he'd debated long and hard before he'd approached his parents. He hadn't wanted to make them feel like he was rejecting them. The words had still been making their way out of his mouth when his mother had shushed him, pulling him into her familiar embrace.

His father had patted him on his shoulder, something he'd done for years as a way of conveying his affection. "We know that, son. Nothing and nobody will ever be able to change the love between us. But we also know that you want to know more about your birth parents. We'll help you in any way that we can."

"I have all of the paperwork from your adoption," his mother had added. "Let me get the file and we can go through it together."

Just like that, all of Caleb's worries had vanished. He'd known that finding his birth father wouldn't break the bond he and his parents shared, but confirmation had gone a long way toward putting him at ease.

His mother had gone into her office, a room decorated in soothing creams with black accents, and returned holding a large manila folder. "This is everything we know about your birth parents."

"Do you want to read it alone or would you like company?" his father asked.

"I'm not sure." He'd wanted to read everything alone,

just in case there was something in there that would break his heart. The last thing he wanted was for his parents to witness his pain. At the same time, he'd needed their support.

"How about we let you read everything on your own first," his mother had said after a moment. "If you have any questions or want to talk about anything, we'll be here."

"That sounds like a good plan," Caleb had agreed.

The only problem was there had been no new information in the file. He still knew only that his mother was deceased, and his father had wanted to maintain his anonymity. Caleb had tried to get his original birth certificate, but he hadn't been successful in that either.

His mother had been the one to suggest that he write a letter to his birth father in care of the adoption agency. He'd sent the letter the following day, but weeks later he hadn't gotten a response. With each passing day, his hope of hearing from his biological father dwindled. As a last desperate measure, he'd tried one of those DNA tests, hoping to find a relative that way, but had come up empty. If he had any biological family, they weren't trying to figure out where they'd come from. But then, they probably already knew.

He'd come up against an impenetrable brick wall and had been ready to admit defeat when pictures of Brooks Langtree had sprung up all around Montana. No matter where Caleb went, he couldn't escape the image. There was a resemblance between the two that couldn't be denied. Since he was all out of options, he'd decided to try to meet with Brooks Langtree and get his question answered.

Was Brooks his biological father? The resemblance between the two had made Caleb believe it was possible. But the more he learned about Brooks Langtree, the less likely it seemed. Brooks didn't seem the type to give away a child and then make it next to impossible to be found.

But then, who knew the kind of person he'd been thirty years ago. Langtree was a good-looking man, even at fifty. He'd probably been even more so in his youth. No doubt he'd had women chasing after him at twenty. After all, he had been a rising star with a bright future. That would make him even more appealing to a whole segment of women. Perhaps a rodeo groupie had gotten pregnant. Perhaps once she'd died, Brooks Langtree hadn't wanted the responsibility of raising a child on his own.

Caleb shook his head. He'd promised himself not to let his imagination run wild. He would deal with facts, and *only* facts. If he couldn't prove a theory, then he would discard it. That was the only way to ensure that he didn't travel down the wrong path, ending up farther away from the truth than he was now.

Pulling out his phone, he punched in his parents' number. He was a grown man, but he still turned to them for support and advice.

After two rings, his mother's familiar voice came over the line. Although Caleb had lived in his own place ever since he'd graduated from college, he saw his parents all the time. They were just as close as ever.

"How are you, son?" Iris asked. That was the first question she'd asked him for as long as he could remember. The first thing she'd always wanted to know.

"I'm actually good," Caleb said. He might not have stood face-to-face with Brooks Langtree, but he had seen close-up images of the man on the video screen. There was enough of a resemblance for Caleb to believe they could be related.

But that wasn't the only reason Caleb was so elated. The other reason was Faith Hawkins. Just being around her had made him feel emotions he hadn't experienced in a long time—if ever. She was so easy to be with. So much fun. She was a light that brightened dark places in his heart. Being with her felt good. It felt right. Although he hadn't been looking for a romantic entanglement when he'd come to Bronco—and he still wasn't—meeting Faith had been an unexpected bonus.

He wished he'd made plans to see her again. He'd had a chance when she'd texted him to let him know she had arrived home safely but he hadn't taken it. Instead of setting up another date, he'd wished her good-night and sweet dreams. He was on a mission and couldn't allow himself to be distracted.

"Hold on so your father can pick up the extension," Iris said.

Her muffled voice came over the phone as she covered the receiver with her hand and called for her husband to get on the phone. Caleb couldn't help but smile to himself. Although his parents had cell phones, they insisted on keeping their landline. After a moment his father's voice came over the phone. "How are things going?"

"Everything's fine."

"Did you get a chance to meet with Brooks Langtree?"

It was just like his father to get to the heart of the matter. Nathan believed in facing a problem head-on. Get it all out there and find a solution. That was his motto.

"No. But I didn't really expect to. I just wanted to see the man in the flesh instead of just looking at pictures."

"And?"

"The resemblance is there. The pictures didn't lie. He might be my biological father."

"Don't get your hopes up," Iris cautioned. "Even if that's true. You might be excited to meet him, but he might not feel the same."

"I know." The idea stung, but it couldn't be denied.

"I don't want to have to hurt that man if he hurts my baby," Iris continued.

Caleb and Nathan laughed. Iris talked tough, but she was the sweetest person in the world. Of course, nobody had ever hurt someone she loved.

"I'll keep that in mind," Caleb said.

"So you only saw him from a distance?" Nathan asked.

"Yes. On the big screen."

"So why are you in such a good mood?" Iris asked.

Was he going to mention Faith? After all, there wasn't that much to tell. And then there was the risk that his mother would jump to conclusions. Iris was normally a rational person and never allowed her feelings to get the best of her. Unless the topic was romance. Then her brain short-circuited, and logic was replaced by emotions.

It hadn't always been that way. Then about four or five years ago, her friends' children began getting married and having babies. Caleb had always dated, but never seriously. That was no longer good enough for his mother. Suddenly Iris was all about Caleb finding a nice girl, getting serious and settling down. She wanted grandchildren while she was young enough to enjoy them.

"I made a friend. We hung out a little bit and went out to dinner."

"Would this be a female friend?" His mother's voice was filled with hope.

"Iris," Nathan said with a chuckle. "You aren't going to start that, are you? With everything going on, Caleb doesn't have time to focus on romance."

Caleb appreciated his father's support, but knew it was futile. Reasoning wasn't going to work with his mother.

"Caleb is a bright boy. He has the ability to multitask."

Nathan and Caleb laughed again. Iris was on a mission and nothing would deter her.

"Tell me about this girl," Iris said.

"There's not much to tell. Her name is Faith. She competes in rodeo."

"That can be dangerous," Iris said.

"She knows what she's doing. I saw her in action this afternoon. She's really good."

"Does she have to travel a lot?" Nathan asked. "That can be hard on a relationship."

"I don't know how much travelling she has to do. I do know that she toured South America with her sisters not too long ago."

"I didn't know that rodeo was popular all over the world," Nathan said.

"I didn't either," Caleb admitted. There was a lot he didn't know. But if he was going to get closer to Faith, that would need to change.

"Maybe you should think about meeting a girl with

a less dangerous job," Iris said softly. "And one who doesn't travel as much."

"I'm not thinking about marrying Faith, Mom. I just met her a few hours ago."

"That's time enough to know if there was a spark," Nathan said. His mother might be the one urging Caleb to settle down, but his father was the more romantic of the two.

Nathan remembered the exact date and time he and Iris met. He vividly recalled every detail of her outfit down to the earrings and bracelet she'd worn. Nathan often surprised Iris with jewelry, flowers and other *just because* gifts. He was the one who scheduled twice-monthly date nights and romantic weekend getaways for the couple.

"That's true," Caleb conceded. It was useless to argue. Especially since his father was right.

"So, was there a spark?" Nathan asked.

Caleb could evade the question, but he wouldn't. Even though he wasn't looking for a relationship, for some odd reason he wanted his parents to know about Faith. "There was. I can't explain it. I've been attracted to women before, of course, but what I felt for Faith was different. Stronger."

"She could be the one," Nathan said.

"Don't jump to conclusions," Iris said. "He barely knows her."

"And she might travel for her dangerous job," Caleb said, voicing his mother's true concern.

"Exactly."

"What else do you know about her?" Nathan asked.

"Not much." He could tell his parents that she was petite with the sexiest body that he had ever seen. Or that she had a sultry voice, a happy laugh, and smelled like Heaven, but he knew that wasn't the kind of thing they wanted to know. "Oh. I do know a bit about her family. Her grandmother was a big star in rodeo a while ago. Hattie Hawkins. And Faith's mother and aunts used to compete as the Hawkins Sisters."

"Faith is a Hawkins?" Iris asked.

"Yes. Does that make a difference?"

"Of course it does. Anyone with even a passing knowledge of rodeo knows about Hattie Hawkins. She helped to make rodeo safer and more humane. She had great influence in her day. She still does. Her daughters were very talented and skilled. They're all very professional. From what I hear, this new generation is just as talented. They generally win their events, but they never take foolish risks."

"So I take it that you're no longer opposed to me spending time with Faith," Caleb said.

"No. Not that I thought it would make a difference. You're your father's son when it comes to romance. Stubborn as a mule. Besides, if Faith is a Hawkins, I know she'll be careful. And I know that I'll like her."

Caleb smiled at the not-so-subtle hint. Now that Iris approved of Faith, it was full steam ahead. Iris was ready to march him down the aisle this year and help him build a nursery the next. "Slow down, Mom. It was only one date. Besides, I'm focused on finding out if Brooks Langtree is my biological father. If so, the search is over. If not, I need to keep looking. Until this is settled, I'm not in a position to start a relationship."

"Humph," Iris replied, clearly displeased by his answer.

"What's your plan for tomorrow?" Nathan asked.

"I'm going to try to meet with Brooks Langtree. I just have to figure out a way to make that happen."

"Is there anything I can do to help?"

"No, Dad. Thanks for offering. I'll find a way." He hoped.

"Good. I hope he can give you the answer you're looking for."

"So do I."

Faith leaned against the back of the tub, then sank down until the warm, sudsy water brushed against her chin. Closing her eyes, she let the sound of the saxophone playing over the speaker wash over her. Nothing soothed her like a long, scented bubble bath accompanied by smooth jazz, especially after a day of competition. Though today had simply been an exhibition, her muscles still appreciated the relaxing bath.

Brooks Langtree Day had been great. Faith had enjoyed seeing the older man get the recognition he deserved. He had grinned the entire time, joy bursting from every pore as the crowd acknowledged his accomplishments. But that hadn't been the best part of her day. Nor had being serenaded by the audience, although that had unexpectedly been fun. Meeting Caleb had been the highlight of the day.

He was by far the most interesting man she'd met in years. He had a quick sense of humor and an easygoing demeanor that made him fun to be around. His handsome face and muscular body appealed to her on a basic level. In simple terms, he was good to look at.

That thought made her laugh. How many times had

she said that she wanted men to look at her as a person and not focus so much on her looks? Yet here she was, doing the same thing to Caleb. Oh, well. Life was like that sometimes.

She'd really enjoyed herself tonight. Everything had been perfect. The burger, fries and shake had hit the spot. Walking around town and sharing some of her favorite spots with Caleb had been fun. She remembered how impressed she'd been when she'd seen Bronco for the first time. How at home she'd felt. There was something about Bronco that felt familiar. Every person was so warm and welcoming. The town was like a big hug. She wondered if Caleb had felt the same way. Not that it mattered. He hadn't given any indication that he was looking for a new hometown.

Faith soaked until the water turned chilly and her bubbles had faded away. Then she dried off on a fluffy towel, smoothed on her favorite scented lotion and put on a pair of orange pajamas. She had just settled in her bed with a cup of tea and a mystery novel when her phone rang. She glanced at the screen and smiled.

"Hi, Elizabeth. What are you doing up this late?"

"I finally have a moment of quiet. The kids are asleep and I decided to give you a call to see how your date went."

"It wasn't a date," Faith was quick to point out.

"Did you prearrange a time and place to meet?"

"Yes."

"Did you have an established agenda?"

Faith sighed. She knew where Elizabeth was going. She also knew that Elizabeth was relentless and there was no way to stop her. "Also yes."

"Then it was a date."

"Okay, smarty-pants. It was a date."

"And? How did it go?"

"It was wonderful," Faith said. If she'd thought before answering, she might have been less effusive. She didn't want to give her sister the wrong idea. Not that she thought Elizabeth would jump to conclusions. Her sister was well aware that Faith wasn't looking for love. Once burned, lesson learned.

"Oh. *Wonderful*," Elizabeth echoed. "Tell me more."

Faith piled her pillows behind her back and then sighed. "There's not much to tell. We walked around town for a bit and then stopped for burgers and shakes."

"Ah. Dinner."

Faith rolled her eyes. "Why are you so determined to make a bigger deal out of this than it is?"

"I'm not. I'm simply summing up what you're saying."

"No. You're spinning what I'm saying. You're in love, so now you have romance on the brain."

"That could be true. Remember what I told you when Jake and I started dating. Your Mr. Wonderful could be right around the corner. Who knows, it could be Caleb."

"We just met."

"But do you like him?"

Faith smiled. "I do. I felt really comfortable with him."

"I knew it," Elizabeth crowed. "I had a good feeling about the two of you."

"Don't get ahead of yourself. I'm perfectly content to take things slowly."

"Even that is a big change for you. Before you met

Caleb you weren't willing to even think about having a relationship."

"Right. So don't make me nervous or I might turn tail and run."

Elizabeth laughed. "I'm not worried about that. You've never run away from anything in your life. Especially not a man."

"There's always a first time."

"And," Elizabeth continued as if Faith's words weren't worthy of acknowledgement, much less a reply, "you have never run away from happiness."

"You sound so sure that Caleb is offering me happiness." Of course, there was no reason for her to suspect that Caleb would bring her unhappiness. He'd been so honest and open today. People who were up to no good generally weren't so forthcoming.

That sliver of doubt returned to nag at Faith. She still suspected that Caleb was holding something back. She believed him when he said that it wasn't another woman. Even if he was withholding something, so what? She didn't expect him to bare his soul to her on their first date. There was a time and a place for everything. An order to things. Too much information might have sent her running for the hills. They were still in the getting-to-know-each-other phase of their relationship. If indeed there was a relationship. They hadn't made plans to see each other again, so she could be worrying about nothing.

But they could get together. Caleb was staying in town this weekend. And she had his phone number. She could call him. But when she'd texted him that she was home, his answer had been perfunctory. He hadn't made an effort to get a conversation started. But then, neither had she.

"I don't know what he's offering you," Elizabeth said honestly, pulling Faith's attention back to the conversation. "But I do know that life seldom goes according to our plans. My life is proof of that. Bad things happen. I lost Arlo to an undiagnosed heart condition with no warning. I didn't think I would ever recover emotionally or that I would be able to love again. But I did. Sometimes good things are waiting to happen. All we have to do is be open to them."

"That sounds so easy."

"It is. The question you need to answer is this: Are you willing?"

"I don't know," Faith admitted.

"And on that note, I'm going to say good-night," Elizabeth said. "Morning comes early around here."

Elizabeth's words echoed in Faith's head long after they'd ended the call. Something good could be waiting for her right around the corner. All she had to do was be open to it.

Was she willing to take a chance and possibly find love?

Chapter Four

Caleb stared at his phone. For the past ten minutes he'd been debating with himself, trying to decide whether or not to reach out to Faith. Today was the second day of the Golden Buckle Rodeo and Caleb expected Brooks Langtree to be in attendance. If he was there, Caleb might have a chance to talk with him. Even with that idea in mind, Caleb couldn't stop thinking about Faith. But should he call her? Or should he stay focused on the task at hand and the reason he was in Bronco?

Debate over, he tapped in her number and waited while the phone rang. There really hadn't been much doubt what he was going to do. The minute the notion struck him, he'd known he would eventually break down and reach out to her. He reasoned that if she hadn't wanted him to call her, she wouldn't have given him her number.

"Hi, Caleb. What's up?" Faith's voice was slightly breathless as if she had been running. Hopefully, he hadn't interrupted something important.

"I was just wondering if you would be interested in going to dinner with me tonight." That wasn't exactly why he'd been calling, but he did want to see her. Besides, he had no idea how she would react if he told her that he'd thought about her all night and had longed to hear her voice from the moment he'd awakened this morning. He was probably better off not saying that he wanted to spend time with her to find out if the feelings she'd stirred in him yesterday were real and just how deep they went. No, asking for a date was much more appropriate.

"I would like that very much," Faith said. "Where do you want to go?"

"Let me do some checking and get back to you."

"Oh, a man who is willing to do some research about the town. I like that."

His heart warmed at the pleasure in her voice. He'd learned from watching his father that when it came to women, the little things were actually the big things. "What time is good for you?"

"I'm free around seven," she said.

"I'll call you around six if that works for you."

"It does. I'll talk to you then."

After the call ended, Caleb smiled. Although there was still a lot unsettled in his life, just talking to Faith made his concerns seem that much smaller. That thought brought him up short. Faith shouldn't be able to impact his mood like that. And yet she had.

Deciding that this was a puzzle to solve at another time, Caleb grabbed his Stetson and jacket, then headed downstairs. The B and B provided breakfast for the guests of course, but Caleb was suddenly much too edgy to sit down to eggs and bacon. That would consume too much time.

Grabbing a bagel and an apple from the buffet set

up in the dining room, Caleb nodded at Claire and left. He took a big bite from the juicy fruit and then headed to the convention center. When Caleb arrived, Brooks Langtree and his people were already in place, seated in their private box away from the crowd. Disappointment that he wouldn't have a chance to "bump into" Langtree swamped Caleb and for a moment he considered leaving. He shoved the idea down. It wasn't his nature to give up without even trying. He would create an opportunity to meet the man. That decided, he found his seat and then looked over the program. Today's exhibition was limited to the men.

Caleb flashed back to Faith's appearance yesterday. She'd been impressive. Masterful. It had been a pleasure to watch as she confidently circled the barrels placed around the ring. She'd steered her horse very close to the barrels, but never once had either she or the horse touched one. When she'd finished her ride, the crowd had risen to its collective feet and given her a well-earned standing ovation.

Caleb had never cared much about rodeo. Before yesterday, he had never attended an event nor watched one on TV. He was a football fan. Even with his lack of knowledge, he could tell when someone was merely good as opposed to being exceptional. Faith fit firmly in the latter category. But she wasn't the reason he was here today, he reminded himself. Brooks Langtree was.

The lights dimmed and the crowd cheered. An unseen announcer welcomed everyone to the second day of the Golden Buckle Rodeo. He then acknowledged Brooks Langtree, who waved to the crowd from the VIP section. Although it made no sense, Caleb waved back.

The cowboys came out and began to compete in the first event. Caleb was impressed by the skill the riders displayed as they took turns lassoing a running calf while remaining on horseback. When that event ended, the next one started. Caleb was surprised to find himself on his feet cheering when riders managed to stay on the back of a spinning and bucking bull for eight seconds. This weekend was turning him into a rodeo fan.

When the rodeo ended, the lights came up. Caleb turned and looked to the VIP section. Brooks Langtree and his party were leaving their private box. Perhaps if he hurried, Caleb could catch him backstage.

Caleb went against the tide of the exiting crowd and worked his way backstage. As he grew closer to the stage door, his heart began to pound and sweat beaded on his forehead. Was he about to meet his biological father? What would they say to each other? Would Brooks Langtree be happy to be reunited with the son he'd given up for adoption three decades ago? Or would he be angry that Caleb had managed to track him down? Would he say that he'd made it clear that he wanted the adoption to remain closed because he had no interest in ever seeing Caleb again? That horrible thought stopped Caleb in his tracks and he considered turning around and leaving.

Caleb took a steadying breath and ordered himself to slow down. He was making a huge leap here. There was still no proof that Brooks Langtree was his father. He needed to discover that first. Caleb started walking again, not stopping until he reached the backstage door. A security guard blocked entry.

"How can I help you?" The guard didn't smile, but he didn't appear particularly menacing either.

Caleb didn't know why he had expected to just walk up and talk to Brooks Langtree. He should have anticipated encountering a barrier. This may be a town with friendly people, but security was a necessity everywhere these days. Not to mention that Brooks Langtree was a celebrity.

"I was hoping to meet Brooks Langtree."

"I see. And is he expecting you?" The guard picked up a clipboard and glanced at a paper secured there. Caleb knew his name wouldn't be on any list.

"No."

"Are you a reporter?"

"No."

The guard gave Caleb a searching look. Perhaps he saw something on his face, because he held up a hand. "Hold on a minute. Obviously I can't let you past. But Mr. Harvey, Mr. Langtree's agent, is coming this way. You can speak with him."

Caleb looked over the guard's shoulder at a well-dressed older man who was striding in their direction. He held a cell phone pressed to his ear and appeared to be listening intently to whoever was on the other end. The guard waved at the man, who nodded. When he finished his conversation, he slipped the phone into his jacket pocket and strode over to them.

"What can I do for you?" the agent asked the guard.

"Mr. Harvey, this young man wants to meet with Mr. Langtree."

"I see." The agent gave him a once-over. "Are you a reporter?"

"No." Caleb and the guard answered at the same time.

"What business do you have with Mr. Langtree?"

Caleb hesitated. “It’s personal.”

“Is that right?” Mr. Harvey sucked his teeth.

“Yes.”

“I handle Mr. Langtree’s business affairs.”

“If this was a business affair, I would talk to you. But it’s not. It’s personal,” Caleb said firmly, hoping that answer would be good enough for the man. Caleb couldn’t just blurt out that he might be Brooks Langtree’s son. Especially since he wasn’t sure it was true.

“I don’t think you understand, son,” Mr. Harvey said quietly. “Nobody gets to see Mr. Langtree without going through me.”

Caleb bit back his frustration and swallowed harsh words. Being rude wouldn’t accomplish anything other than getting him kicked out of the building.

“I get it. I do. And I’m not trying to be difficult. The matter I was hoping to speak to him about is personal. I’m not sure he would want anyone else to hear.”

The security guard and the agent exchanged glances and all friendliness vanished. Mr. Harvey’s slightly impatient expression morphed into one of undisguised suspicion and hostility. Clearly they were protective of Mr. Langtree.

“Is that supposed to be some kind of a threat?” Mr. Harvey asked. His voice was hard and his eyes narrowed into slits.

“Not at all,” Caleb said quickly, hastening to erase the impression he’d just made and defuse the tense situation. “It’s nothing like that. Look, I just need ten minutes alone with him.”

“As I said earlier, that’s not going to happen,” Mr. Harvey said. “Now, if you’re not going to tell me what you want, there is no need to continue this conversation." The agent pulled out his phone, tapped in a number and walked away.

"That didn't go the way I'd hoped," Caleb muttered to himself.

"No, I imagine it didn't."

Caleb jumped. For a moment there, he'd forgotten that the security guard was still around. Not that it mattered. He'd already gotten the only answer he was going to get.

"I just need to meet with him."

"Good luck with that," the guard said dryly.

"Yeah." Caleb walked away. That was a bust. He needed to regroup and come up with a better plan. Actually, this hadn't been much of a plan. Did he think that he was just going to walk up to a rodeo legend and have a private conversation about a secret child? He must have been delusional.

When he reached the parking lot, Caleb leaned against his truck and looked up. One big puffy cloud floated in the clear blue sky. When Caleb had been a kid, he and his father used to go on fishing trips to a lake near Tenacity. While waiting for the fish to bite, they would point out shapes in the clouds. Those had been great times and Caleb smiled at the happy memories. More often than not, they hadn't caught more than two or three fish between them. Without exception, Nathan had taken one look and declared the fish was too small—no matter how big the fish looked to Caleb—and said that they needed to throw it back.

Caleb was thirteen before he realized that while Nathan enjoyed their father-and-son time, he wasn't a fan of fishing. Or more accurately, he didn't like the idea of killing the fish. His big, strong father had a heart as mushy as a marshmallow. Caleb loved that about Nathan. His father wasn't embarrassed to show his gentler side. He had never tried to make Caleb into a hard man. Nathan let Caleb know that it was okay to cry when he was sad and that it was perfectly fine to experience every emotion, even the softer ones. Especially the softer ones.

Although Nathan had assured him that he wasn't being unfaithful by seeking out his birth father, Caleb still felt as if he was being disloyal to the man who'd raised him with such love. The man who had patiently taught him how to knot a tie, listened as he cried over a girl who had broken his heart, and taught him how to drive a stick shift.

Given the love that Nathan had shown him, why was Caleb consumed with the need to know more about his birth father? Meeting him wasn't going to change anything. Caleb wasn't going to start turning to his biological dad for advice. He wasn't going to start confiding in him about his hopes and dreams. No man would never replace Nathan Strom in Caleb's life or affection. So why was he so determined to meet his birth father if he didn't expect anything in his life to change?

What if Brooks Langtree—or whoever Caleb's birth father was—wanted things to change? What if he wanted to have a part in Caleb's life? Would Caleb make a place for him? And how would that make Nathan and Iris feel? Was Caleb opening a can of worms that should remain closed? Caleb loved his parents more than anyone else in the world. He would sacrifice his happiness for them. If they didn't want his biological father to be a part of his life, then no matter how much Caleb wanted to know about his past, Caleb would keep him away. So why was he doing this?

Frowning, he forced the thoughts from his mind. This line of thinking was giving him a headache.

Caleb's stomach growled and he checked his watch. Hours had passed since he'd eaten that apple and bagel, which hadn't been much of a breakfast to begin with. Time enough for him to get good and hungry. He'd spotted a diner in town earlier and been eager to give it a try. Hopping into his truck, he drove there. It was past lunchtime but the dining room was still nearly full.

"Take any table you want and I'll be right with you," the waitress said as Caleb stepped inside the Gemstone Diner. He contemplated taking a seat at the counter since he was alone, but then decided against it. The booth by the windows would be perfect for people-watching. Although he was only in town for a little while, it wouldn't hurt to get a better feel for the place. Especially since Faith had decided to call Bronco home.

What was it about Bronco that appealed to her? It had to be more than the boutiques and eateries. You could find those anywhere. It couldn't be the weather. Winters in Montana could be long and brutal even for the hardiest of souls. That left the people. What characteristics did they share? He didn't expect the answer to show up on their faces—unless you counted the smiles they wore. Maybe that was it. The happiness. The belief the people in town had that tomorrow would be just as good as today if not better. The sense that good things were waiting right around the corner. A feeling that the people of Tenacity seemed to be lacking.

"What will you have?" the waitress asked, standing beside his table. Her name tag read Mandy.

"How is your meat loaf?"

"Just the best in the state," she said with a bright smile.

"You mean, second to my mother's," he said with a grin.

"That goes without saying."

"In that case, I'll have meat loaf."

Mandy took his menu and promised to be back with his meal soon. While he waited, Caleb tried to come up with a new plan for meeting Brooks Langtree. Obviously Brooks's agent wasn't going to allow Caleb to get near him, so he couldn't use the typical lines of communication. Writing a letter was out because he didn't know who would open it. Brooks Langtree might have a person for that. The same was true of an email. Too bad Mr. Harvey had been so protective today.

While Caleb stared out the window, his mind wandered. Naturally he ended up thinking about Faith. He was looking forward to seeing her tonight, but he didn't want to ask her for a restaurant suggestion. He needed to take the initiative so she would know that he cared enough about her to put in the effort.

Mandy set his plate in front of him with a smile. "Here you go. Let me know if I you need anything else."

"Will do."

After the first bite, Caleb leaned back and smiled. The meat loaf was good. While he ate, Caleb tried to come up with a plan for meeting Brooks Langtree. Unfortunately each idea he came up with had too many hurdles and relied upon luck.

"How was it?" Mandy asked, coming up to his table.

"As good as advertised."

Mandy smiled. "Told you."

"Earlier you said I should let you know if I needed anything else."

"Sure." She reached for her pencil and pad. "What else can I get for you?"

"Actually, I would like a bit of help."

"Sure." She put a hand on her hip. "What do you need?"

"This is going to sound odd, but I'm not from here. I live in Tenacity."

"That doesn't sound odd. Lots of people come to Bronco from time to time. Especially when there is a rodeo in town."

"Okay. I'm looking for a place to eat."

She looked around. "I'd say you found one."

He grimaced. "That didn't come out right. I have a date tonight and was looking for a restaurant. Do you have a favorite place?"

She gestured broadly. "Apart from here, you mean?"

"Yeah."

"Depends on your wallet. There's Coeur de l'Ouest, which is quite expensive but worth every penny. Great food. Wonderful ambience. Scenic views. Impeccable service. And there is no way you'll be able to get in without a reservation. It's too late to get one now. There's also the Association. I heard that their food is really good but I've never been there. It's a private club. If you're not a member—"

He held up a hand, stopping her before she could continue. "Maybe I wasn't clear. I'm looking for places that I *can* take a date, not someplace that I *can't*."

She nodded. "If you like Italian, there's Pastabilities.

That's a nice family restaurant and reservations aren't required."

He pictured a lot of kids running around and noise that would probably not be conducive to conversation. "What else do you have?"

"There's always DJ's Deluxe. It's a great rib joint. There's a chance you could get a reservation." She winced. "But it's the weekend, so…"

"You're killing me here. Surely there has to be another option."

"There's another place in town. Lulu's BBQ. It's not fancy, but the food is great."

"How not fancy is it?"

"It's really down-home. Paper towels on the table. That kind of thing."

What would Faith think if he suggested a place like Lulu's BBQ for their first official date, especially since they had gotten burgers and shakes the other day? Would she think he was a cheapskate? He might like Lulu's, but he doubted Faith would be impressed. And he really wanted to impress her.

"Thanks for your suggestions," Caleb said.

"You're welcome." Mandy gave him the bill.

He opened his wallet and pulled out some cash. "Keep the change."

"Thanks. And good luck finding the perfect place for dinner."

It was hard if not impossible to find a place to take a date when you didn't know your way around. Pulling out his phone, he did what he had hoped to avoid. He called Faith for a suggestion.

"Hello," Faith said. At the sound of her voice, Caleb

smiled. There was a slight fluttering in his stomach that startled him. His body had never reacted like that to a woman's voice. Her legs. Yes. Her face. Definitely. But not her voice. "How are you?"

"I could use your help," he admitted.

"Go ahead."

"I know that I told you that I wanted to plan our date but I'm having a bit of trouble finding a restaurant."

She laughed. "So you're telling me that it's hard to find a place to eat in a town that you're not at all familiar with?"

"That about sums it up."

"Good thing I have a couple of ideas."

"Go ahead."

"Lulu's BBQ. It's not fancy but they have the tenderest ribs and the best sauce I have ever tasted."

"I heard about that place. You'd be happy going there for a date?"

"Absolutely. Unless you don't like ribs."

"I love ribs."

"Then it's set."

"You really are a surprise."

"Because I'd rather go to a regular restaurant instead of some hoity-toity place with white linen tablecloths?"

"Well…yeah."

"Don't get me wrong. I like a fancy restaurant just as much as the next girl, but they aren't the only places I go. I go to restaurants for the food. And today I would like to eat ribs. Lulu's are top-tier."

"I like the way you think." He'd been willing to follow the expected playbook when it came to first dates, but it looked like he didn't have to this time.

“That’s a point in your favor,” she said with a laugh.

“Would you like me to pick you up or would you rather meet there?”

“Do you think you know your way around town well enough to find my house?”

“I have GPS.”

“In that case, you should pick me up. It is a date after all.” He smiled at the humor in her voice, a clear sign that he was going to have a great time tonight. “I’ll text you my address.”

“Okay.” His phone buzzed. He looked at the screen. “Got it.”

“Good. Then I’ll see you tonight.”

They ended the call and Caleb’s spirits soared. He might not have gotten the opportunity to meet with Brooks Langtree, but he would be having dinner with Faith.

In his book, that was a win.

Chapter Five

Faith held the phone for a few seconds after she and Caleb ended the conversation. Anticipation flowed through her body and she smiled. She'd dated her share of men, but she'd never felt this attracted to one before. She had never experienced such a strong connection so soon after meeting someone. And she'd certainly never felt such an intense longing to be with anyone. This feeling wasn't entirely comfortable but she couldn't seem to shake it. She wasn't even sure she wanted to.

One thing was certain—she wasn't going to make a big deal of it. Nor was she going to try to figure out what any of this meant. Caleb's six-feet-plus of muscles weren't the only things he had going for him. He was a good man—one she hoped would become a good friend.

Realizing that she was wasting time, she set down the phone and headed to her bathroom. She took a hot shower, using her favorite scented soap that calmed her jumpy nerves. When she was done, she smoothed on lotion and then released her hair from the shower cap. Though she wasn't looking for a relationship, she did enjoy male company. She loved her sisters and cousins and they spent a lot of time together. But there was something different about hanging out with a man. Something special. She liked getting a man's perspective on things. With the right man, discussions could be spirited and fun. Caleb had already shown that he was intelligent and a good conversationalist, so tonight held lots of promise.

Faith also liked dressing up. When she and her female relatives and friends went out, she generally didn't spend a lot of time on her appearance. A bit of lipstick, some mascara and maybe some color on her cheeks and she was ready to go. Even though she and Caleb were going to a casual dinner spot, this was still a date and warranted her full beauty regimen.

Going into her bedroom, she slipped on her silk underwear and then a satin robe. Taking her time, she dabbed on foundation, brushed on blush and eye shadow. She put on mascara and lipstick and then smiled at her reflection, pleased by what she saw. She pulled on her new purple blouse, tight black jeans and boots and spritzed on her favorite perfume. She had just put on silver earrings and bangles when her doorbell rang.

She glanced at the clock on her bedside table. Right on time. Grabbing her purse, she descended the stairs and headed for the front door. She swung it open and barely managed to hold back a gasp when she saw Caleb.

Dressed in a white long-sleeved pullover that hugged his broad shoulders and solid chest before it tapered to his flat stomach, and faded jeans that emphasized his muscular thighs, he was temptation on two legs. Telling herself not to make a fool of herself by drooling, she held the door open so he could enter.

"Thank you." He stepped into the room and she tried to see it through his eyes. The eclectic space had been designed for comfort, not fashion. She'd furnished her house with items that she had accumulated on her travels over the years. Each knickknack, piece of furniture and rug held special meaning for her.

"I'm ready. I just need to grab a jacket," she said, heading for the closet.

"Take your time." He looked around. "I don't know what I was expecting, but this room suits you perfectly."

"How so?"

"It's a little bit of everything." He gestured first to her large, striped sofa with its carved wooden arms before pointing to the tan leather chair with the blue striped throw draped across the back. Then he pointed to the miniature carved figures serving as bookends for her signed novels. "The pieces are a bit different from each other, and not at all what you would see anywhere else. Everything is unique. Just like you. And they all belong together, working together to create one cozy room. I like it."

"You totally get my style." In a way, he had summed up her personality. She wasn't predictable. She had lots of different facets. Not that she was going to let him know that. She needed to keep him guessing, at least for a while. Especially since there was still something mysterious about him. Of course, that could be her overactive imagination at work. Perhaps she should lay off the mystery books and movies and replace them with comedies.

Caleb helped her put on her jacket and they stepped onto her front porch. Once the door was locked behind them, they walked to his pickup and climbed in.

"Nice," Faith said, touching the butter-soft leather seats.

"I spend a lot of time on the road for the store. I'm either visiting customers, in search of new ones, or meeting with suppliers, so I need a comfortable ride."

This top-of-the-line vehicle was definitely that. It had all of the bells and whistles including a few features she had never seen before and wouldn't mind having in her car.

Lulu's BBQ was only a short ride away, so they were only able to discuss surface topics before he was parking in the lot behind the red brick building. Faith looked forward to having more in-depth conversations as they ate.

"You are going to love this place so much," Faith said as they walked through the door. The aroma of smoked meat, spicy sauce and frying potatoes filled the air, and she inhaled deeply.

"It smells so good I'm already in love," Caleb said.

There were lots of people in the dining room, and they had to wait for a few minutes for a vacant table. Disco music from the seventies played on invisible speakers and Faith tapped her toes to the beat.

Once a table had been cleared, Caleb pulled out the padded stool for Faith and then took the seat across from her. Instead of placemats, there were brown paper napkins on the wooden table. Where other restaurants had autographed photos of celebrities who'd dined at their establishment on their walls, Lulu had framed pictures of the smoking process on hers. Clearly she was as proud of her food as other restaurant owners were of their famous customers.

Caleb and Faith pulled laminated menus from between the paper napkin holder and the salt and pepper shakers and perused them. Patrons could order a meal by the number or create one from the slabs, tips, sandwiches and variety of sides on offer. A waitress dressed in black jeans, a white shirt and an apron with Lulu's logo embroidered on the top approached them. She set tumblers of ice water on the table, then grabbed a pencil and pad of paper from her apron pocket. She smiled at them. "Are you ready to order?"

Caleb and Faith exchanged glances. She nodded. "Yes."

They placed their orders and then the waitress nodded. "I'll be right back with your drinks."

Once they were alone, Faith turned back to Caleb. She had a million questions, so she voiced the first ones that came to her mind. "What brings you to Bronco? Are you trying to get more business for your store? Will you be coming back?"

Caleb took a swallow of water as he tried to decide how to answer those questions. He was always looking for more customers, so he could say yes. It wouldn't be a lie, but it wouldn't be the truth either. He didn't want to deceive Faith. But he didn't want to tell her that he believed Brooks Langtree was his birth father. "I was hoping to get a feel for rodeo. I've never been a fan, even living in Montana, believe it or not, and Brooks Langtree Day seemed to be a good opportunity to see it up close. He is something of a legend. Being in his presence was special."

"Judging by the turnout, a lot of people felt the same way. I'm glad that people came to show their appreciation for all that he's done in his career. He helped pave the way for lots of today's competitors."

"I know. And it turns out that I got to sit with one of those competitors. But that's not the only reason I came to Bronco."

"No?"

He inhaled deeply and then blew out a slow breath. He couldn't believe it, he certainly hadn't planned it, but he was going to tell Faith the truth. Though he hadn't known her long, he could tell that she was a good person. A trustworthy person. Even so, he needed her to know how serious the matter was. And he needed to make sure he wouldn't be overheard. The restaurant was a good size and all of the tables were occupied. Fortunately, there was lots of space between the tables. Not only that, the other diners were talking to each other. Nobody was paying the least bit of attention to Faith and Caleb.

"You seem to be struggling," Faith said. "Feel free to tell me however much or how little you feel comfortable sharing. Or we can change the subject entirely."

Before he could reply, the waitress set their meals in front of them. After giving them extra napkins and containers of sauce, she excused herself and walked away. By unspoken agreement, Caleb and Faith each tasted their rib tips. A groan of pleasure slipped through his lips. "This is so good. I might never be the same."

Faith grinned. "I told you that you'd like it."

"Don't tell my dad, who is the grill master in our family, but these are the best ribs I have ever tasted."

Faith pretended to lock her lips and the action drew his attention to her full mouth. It looked so soft he longed to press his lips to hers in a hot kiss in order to find out if it was as soft as it looked. "Lots of people feel the same way. Even so, Caleb, your secret is safe with me."

He hoped so, because he was about to share another secret. “You asked why I was here in Bronco.”

“I did. But I didn’t mean to pry.”

“You didn’t. The truth is…” His voice trailed off. The words were harder to say than he’d expected. Once he’d said them, there would be no taking them back. Exhaling a deep breath, he forced out the words. “I’m here looking for my birth father.”

“Okay.” She nodded as if what he’d just said wasn’t a big deal. Maybe to her it wasn’t.

“I’m adopted,” he repeated, just in case she needed clarification.

“So am I.”

“You are?” His mouth dropped open.

“Yes. So are my sisters and many of my cousins. My mother and her sisters are adopted too.”

“I didn’t know that.”

She gave him a wide smile. “You really aren’t into rodeo, are you?”

“No. But what does that have to do with anything?”

“Our adoptions aren’t a secret. They really couldn’t be, since we’re not all the same race or ethnicity. My mother is white, two of her sisters are Black, and one is Latina. Same with my sisters. Elizabeth and I are Black, Amy and Tori are white, and Carly is Latina.”

“Sorry. I’m more of a football fan,” he admitted with a half smile.

She laughed. “That’s no skin off my nose. But if you aren’t interested in rodeo, and clearly don’t know much about rodeo riders, why were you so intent on seeing Brooks Langtree?”

He didn’t want to lie, but he wasn’t ready to mention

his belief that Brooks Langtree might be his father, just in case he was wrong. "I was given up for adoption thirty years ago. I have reasons to believe my father was on the rodeo circuit thirty years ago. I figured a lot of old-timers might show up to the event. Maybe one of them would have known him."

She nodded slowly as if considering what he'd said. "That's possible, I suppose. But lots of people travel the rodeo circuit. Take it from me, a rider could be here one day and in another town the next. That's the nature of the beast."

"I have to start somewhere. My hometown is only a hundred miles away, so here seems as good a place as any. I don't have any facts to back up my belief. I'm still in search mode."

"What are you looking at? If you don't mind my asking."

"I don't mind at all. It's nice to be able to talk to you about this, especially since we're in the same boat."

She tilted her head and her dark hair drifted over her shoulder. "What do you mean?"

"You're adopted too."

"Yes. But mine was an open adoption. I know who my birth mother is."

"Oh." He felt a twinge of envy, which was ridiculous. "Is she a part of your life?"

Faith shrugged. "Yes and no. I see her from time to time and we email occasionally, but she has her own family and I have mine. She's married and she and her husband have two sons. And I'm a Hawkins through and through. They're my family."

"I understand that. And I feel the same way about my parents."

"That said," Faith continued, "I think I would wonder about her if I didn't know her. That knowledge has kept me from having a lot of unanswered questions."

"That's it exactly. I'm not looking for a new family. Or even to be a part of my biological father's life. I just want to meet him so I can find out about him. Hopefully, he'll tell me something about my birth mother. All I know is that she died when I was a baby." He sighed. "Maybe I'm barking up the wrong tree. He might not have anything to do with rodeo. That's just a guess." He shook his head. "You probably think I'm being ridiculous. And maybe I am."

She grabbed his hand and gave it an urgent squeeze. "Don't do that, Caleb. Don't put yourself down. Whatever you feel is totally understandable. Naturally you want to know where you came from."

"That's just it. I've always known I was adopted. My parents called me their chosen child. I never thought about my biological father until I turned thirty. Then it was like a switch flipped on. It was all that I could think about and I became curious about my past. What were my birth parents like? I know my mom died, but is my father still alive? Does he wonder about me? Does he wish he had kept in touch with me?"

She nodded, sympathy in her eyes. "Do you know anything else about your birth parents?"

"I only know that my father insisted that the adoption be closed. He didn't want me to be given any information about either of them."

"That's not a lot to go on."

"I know." He swallowed some of his cola, trying to wash away the disappointing reality. Because the truth was if Brooks Langtree wasn't his dad, Caleb really had no other clues to follow.

"So, what's your plan?" she asked quietly.

He sighed, forcing down the nagging stress that was never far from him. "I don't have one. If you have an idea, feel free to share it. I'm open to suggestions."

"Nothing comes to mind right now, but if I think of something, I'll let you know."

"Thanks. I mean that sincerely. I feel better now that I've told you."

"Do your parents know that you're looking for your bio dad?"

"Yes. They say they're okay with it."

She gave him a searching look. "Do you believe them?"

"For the most part. I know they would never stand in my way of doing something that I need to do. My happiness matters to them." He grimaced. "But it can't be easy on them. They've had me all to themselves for thirty years. I don't want them to worry about losing their place in my life."

"I don't know your parents, but I doubt they're worried about that."

"How do you know that?"

She smiled gently. "Because as you've said, they've been your parents for thirty years. The love you all share won't vanish simply because you meet the man responsible for half of your genes."

"They said the same thing, although they said it slightly differently."

"Then you know I'm right. So take them at their word."

He took a swallow of his cola and then looked into her eyes. “How does your adoptive mother feel about your birth mother? Does it hurt her when your birth mother comes around?”

“I don’t think so,” she said slowly. “But our situations are not the same. They met before I was born. My birth mother actually chose my parents. I think they feel grateful to her.”

Caleb frowned. “I don’t think my parents will feel gratitude if they meet my biological dad.”

“Are you planning on making him a part of your life?”

“I haven’t thought that far in advance,” he admitted. “To be honest, it depends on him. Just meeting him and getting a few questions answered might be enough.”

“*Might* be enough?”

He shrugged. “I don’t know how I’ll feel. Will just having him acknowledge me and tell me why he gave me away be enough? Is it enough for you?”

“My birth parents were teenagers,” she said, with a half smile. “They were still in high school when my bio mom got pregnant. Their parents convinced them that it would be best for me if they gave me up for adoption. Best for them too. My birth mom insisted on an open adoption so she could always know where I was and that I was okay.”

“You mentioned your birth mother. What about your birth father? Are you in touch with him?”

Faith shook her head, sending her hair cascading over her shoulders. “No. But neither is my birth mom. I guess it was easier for him to walk away and forget I ever existed. Or maybe knowing that I was out there and that he could never be my father was too painful for him. I don't know. Either way, the result is the same."

"Which way do you think my birth father feels?"

She lifted one slender shoulder. "I have no idea. The only way to know for sure is to ask him."

"Which I will do if I find him."

"*When* you find him."

Her confident words comforted him in a way he hadn't expected. Though he'd been uncertain about telling her about his adoption, he was glad that he'd done so. "On that positive note, let's change the subject."

"That works for me. What do you want to talk about?"

"Can you tell me about life on the rodeo circuit?"

"Sure. What do you want to know?"

"Whatever you want to tell me. What are your days like? How does it feel to live and work with the same people that you compete against day after day?"

"They're my friends. Some are my family. I often compete against my cousins and sisters."

"I don't get it. How can you try to beat someone one minute and then act as if you didn't the next? How does that work?"

"It might seem strange to you, but I'm not competing against them. I'm competing against myself. I'm trying to get the best score that I can."

"I get that, but the others are trying to get better scores than you. Someone is going to win and someone is going to lose."

"That's the football fan in you talking. One team battling against the other in a zero-sum game."

"It's competition. Isn't rodeo the same way?"

"Of course, we all want to win. But unlike football,

we're all on the same team. We leave it in the ring. We can root for each other to do well because we're friends. If they do great, it doesn't affect my score. If they do poorly, same thing. My score doesn't change. So I can cheer for them. And they cheer for me. Not only that, we often compete in towns where we don't know anyone else. It would be pretty lonely if we couldn't be friends."

"Everything you're saying makes sense." He admired her even more now. "And it makes me believe that you are one special woman."

Chapter Six

Faith tried not to read too much into Caleb's statement. After all, they'd just had a very emotional conversation. After that personal revelation, his feelings were probably all over the place. The fact that she was sympathetic—indeed empathetic—to his experience had no doubt affected him. He probably didn't mean the words the way they sounded. Even so, her heart was racing.

A moment passed before she realized he was waiting for her reply. "None of what I said makes me special. All the riders on the circuit feel the same way."

"How long do you want to compete?"

"Now, that's a question." She sighed and leaned her chin into her palm. "I've seen so many places and had some wonderful experiences in my travels. I wouldn't have had these experiences without rodeo. I know some people have wanderlust. I'm not one of them. At least not anymore. In fact, I'm turning into quite the opposite. I'm starting to feel the need to put down roots. I'm not thinking about retirement per se. I'm only thirty after all. There are lots of things I still want to do. But I'm thinking about making a few changes in my life."

"You've already made a big one when you moved back to the States."

"That was big," she agreed. "But it was time."

They'd eaten while they'd talked, and now only the bones remained on the plates. Not even one French fry or baked bean had remained uneaten. The waitress returned with their bill, interrupting their conversation. After Caleb paid and left a tip, they exited the restaurant. Faith would have enjoyed lingering for a while, but there was a line of people waiting for the table.

Once they were outside, the subject of her life was dropped and they made small talk on the drive back to her house. Her nerves jangled as they got closer to her block. Although this had been a friendly date, her excitement began to build as she contemplated the way it would end. Would they kiss? Did she want to? Yes and no. Right now she was comfortable with their budding friendship. A kiss, even a perfunctory one at the end of a date, might change that dynamic. Good friends were hard to find, and she didn't want to ruin this friendship by making a mistake. And kissing would definitely be a mistake.

On the other hand, there was no denying the attraction between them. The air practically crackled with sexual tension. Would it be so wrong to act on it just this once in order to see what happened? If they decided that a romantic relationship was wrong for them, they could always take a step back into their old friendship. No harm no foul.

She nearly laughed out loud at the thought. When in the history of the world had that ever happened? Once you stepped over a line, it was impossible to cross back.

"I can practically hear the wheels in your head spinning," Caleb said, bursting into her thoughts. And not a minute too soon.

She turned in her seat so she could look at him while he drove. There was sufficient light from the moon and streetlamps to make his profile visible. With carved cheekbones, full lips and a strong jaw, he was just as attractive in profile as he was straight on. "Is that right?"

"It is."

"Then what am I thinking?"

He grinned, and a dimple appeared. Faith knew there was an equally sexy one in his other cheek. "You're wondering whether you should invite me in when we reach your house. You're also wondering whether I'm going to kiss you good-night."

"Is that right?" She arched an eyebrow.

"Yep."

She decided not to deny it. "Well, are you?"

He laughed. "I'm not going to tell you that now."

"Why not?"

"That would totally ruin the moment. Don't you find the suspense exhilarating?"

She shook her head. "That's one way to describe it."

"What's another?"

She huffed out a breath. "Nerve-wracking."

"Why? It's just a little kiss." He gave her a wicked grin. "What could possibly go wrong?"

"So many things." She pressed her lips together. "That's it. I've decided. I'm not kissing you."

"Wow. That's the first time a woman has said that to me."

"Well, write it down in your diary tonight so you don't forget."

"You think your rejection is something I want to remember?" Caleb asked, an incredulous expression on his face.

"Maybe you should think of this as a learning opportunity."

"What's the lesson? You know, for future reference."

"I'm not sure what you're supposed to learn," she admitted with a wry smile. "When I figure it out, I'll let you know."

"What if I'm not the one who is supposed to learn anything? Perhaps the lesson is yours to learn."

"Maybe. So tell me what bit of wisdom I'm supposed to take from tonight."

He didn't hesitate for a second. "To just go with the flow and not look too far ahead. Don't worry about things that haven't happened yet."

She wondered if he followed that advice. "I'll take that under advisement."

"You do that." Caleb parked in front of her house and turned off the engine.

They got out of the truck and walked side by side up the stairs and to her front door. The sun had long since set and the moon was shining in the starry sky. A gentle breeze blew, knocking a few leaves from the trees lining the street. The wind chime hanging from her porch roof tinkled softly. The night couldn't be more romantic if they were on the set of some romantic movie.

When they reached her front door, they paused and stared into each other's eyes. He was standing so near that Faith actually felt the warmth from his body. Suddenly, she yearned to lean against his muscular chest. Longed to feel his strong arms wrapped around her. Her desire must have shown on her face because he chuckled.

Ever so slowly, he lowered his head until his lips were mere centimeters from hers. Then he froze. "Too bad you decided not to kiss me tonight, because I have a feeling it would have been electric."

Before she could reply, he straightened and took a step back. Eyes dancing mischievously, he held out a hand to her. "Good night, Faith. I had a wonderful time. I would love to see you again when you're available."

"What?" She blinked and sputtered. "What is even happening here?"

"I'm saying good-night to you."

"Oh." She hid her disappointment. He really wasn't going to kiss her.

His cocky grin faded and his expression turned serious. "Thanks for listening to me talk about the search for my biological dad."

"I'm always here if you want to talk."

"I appreciate it." He leaned over and whispered into her ear, "Good night, Faith."

His breath brushed against her neck and her skin tingled. Her knees grew weak and she had no doubt that a kiss would be earth-shattering.

She considered reaching out and pulling his head down to hers while she rose on her tiptoes and kissed him, but before she could act, he turned on his heel and walked down the stairs. Shaking her head in disbelief, she went in the house and leaned against the front door.

Wow. That good-night hadn't gone the way she'd expected. But then, she tried not to have expectations when it came to men. She'd been let down one too many times. It was better to expect nothing and be surprised when something good happened. But Caleb was better than good. He was one of a kind. She'd had so much fun with him and couldn't wait to hang out with him again.

She wasn't one to delude herself about a man's feelings—been there, done that—but she believed that Caleb was as attracted to her as she was to him. And not just physically. She sensed an emotional connection between them. Surprisingly, she wasn't tempted to head to the hills in order to protect herself. She was willing to see where the attraction led. At least for the time being. There was little danger she would fall in love and get hurt while Caleb was trying to find his biological father. That could be a full-time job. Not only that, it had to be emotionally draining, leaving little energy for a romantic relationship.

She recalled his concern for his parents' feelings. Although she'd kept it to herself, she knew they couldn't help but be a little bit hurt even as they supported him. It was only human. Even though her own mother knew Faith loved her to the moon and back, Suzie had admitted to feeling a twinge of jealousy whenever Faith and her birth mother got together. Suzie acknowledged that the problem was hers and that the sensation never lasted long. Gratitude for being chosen as Faith's adoptive mother outweighed the rare negative emotions.

Faith grabbed a glass of water and then checked the time. Suzie was a night owl, so Faith knew she would be awake. Her mother had been on the rodeo tour thirty years ago. Though there were many rodeos going on simultaneously across the country and lots of riders on the circuit, it was still a tight-knit community. Secrets would have been hard to keep. If Caleb's biological dad had actually been on the rodeo circuit back then, her mother might have met him. She might even have known Caleb's birth mother. If she hadn't known either of them, she might have heard some scuttlebutt that could help Caleb fill in some of the blanks. It wouldn't hurt to ask.

She picked up her phone and then punched in her mother's number. Suzie answered on the first ring.

"Hello, my darling daughter," Suzie said. That was her standard greeting for Faith and her sisters and it had been for as long as Faith could remember. There had been a time when Faith had thought her mother called them all "darling daughter" to keep from getting their names mixed up. She wouldn't be the first parent to do that.

When she was fifteen, Faith had asked her mother why she referred to them that way. Even now, recalling Suzie's answer made her smile. "Aren't you my darling daughter? Aren't your sisters? Then why shouldn't I call you that?"

"Hello, my darling mother," Faith replied. She could hear the television in the background. After a moment, the canned laughter vanished, a sign that she had her mother's full attention.

"What are you doing up this late?" Suzie asked. "You always were my early-to-bed, get-up-way-too-early child."

"I just got in from a date."

"Do tell," Suzie said, a smile in her voice.

"Are you sure you want the details?"

"I'm your mother. There's nothing you can't tell

me. Besides, I know you all too well, Faith Clementine Hawkins. I doubt you even kissed the man good-night."

Even now, she still regretted her hastily spoken words. She'd only been teasing. "True."

"Oh ho. And from the disgust and disappointment in your voice, you were hoping for a kiss. That's a surprise."

"Maybe. But that's not why I called."

"Are you sure you didn't call so I could go over and lecture that young man on the proper way to say good-night to a Hawkins woman?"

Faith laughed. "You would, too. I forget how much like Grandma you are."

"I don't see how. My mother raised me to take the bull by the horns."

Faith couldn't stop the groan. "Horrible rodeo pun. When did you start telling dad jokes?"

"I've got talents I have yet to share with the world."

"You might want to keep stand-up comedy to yourself for a wee bit longer."

"I'll admit that wasn't my best material." Suzie chuckled. "Now, if you don't want me to educate your date, how can I help you?"

"Actually, it's my date who needs your help."

"How do you think I can help him?"

Faith hesitated for a moment. "This is confidential."

"Are you asking me to keep this a secret?"

"Yes."

"And did he ask you to keep this a secret?"

"No. I wouldn't say anything to you if he had. But I don't think he wants me blabbing his personal business all over Bronco either. I wouldn't mention it if I didn't think you could help. I know you won't tell anyone."

There was a long pause and Faith knew her mother was giving this matter some thought. Finally, she replied. "All right. Spill."

"Caleb is adopted. He's trying to find his birth father."

"Where is his birth mother? Can't he ask her?"

"No. She'd dead. She died when he was a baby."

"Oh. I'm sorry to hear that." Suzie's voice was filled with sympathy.

"The adoption was closed and the adoption agency won't give him any information. But he wants to find out about his birth father. He wants to meet him if he's still alive."

"How do you think I can help?"

"He thinks his father might have been in the rodeo. Since you were traveling the circuit back then, you might know him."

"Why does he believe that his father was in the rodeo?"

"I don't know. He didn't say. Maybe he pieced that information together over time. Or maybe the adoption agency told him. I didn't want to press him to tell me more than he felt comfortable sharing. But since you were competing all across America thirty years ago, I thought you might have heard some gossip."

"The circuit is quite big," Suzie said slowly. "Hundreds of people participate in almost as many rodeos. You know that."

"I do. But for the most part it's one big family."

"More like a small town made up of several families," Suzie said.

"But still. Word had a way of getting around."

"Giving up a child for adoption is a personal matter, so the people involved are going to be discreet. They might not talk about it to many people outside their immediate family."

"That's true," Faith admitted. "So you didn't hear anything about it?"

"Think, Faith. I was pretty busy thirty years ago. Your father and I had just adopted you. And Elizabeth was already two years old and getting into everything. Tori was ten and was involved in her own activities. I was much too busy raising my family to keep up with the goings-on of the rest of the rodeo circuit."

That made sense, but something in her mother's tone sounded…off. Her voice was strained, as if talking about the subject was uncomfortable. It was more than not liking to talk about adoption or birth parents. Not only that, Suzie loved gossip. Not the mean kind that hurt people. She didn't have time or patience for that kind of nonsense. But even with kids to raise, Suzie had always had her finger on the pulse of the rodeo community. Not much went on that she didn't know about. If someone was looking for a truck or was having trouble making ends meet, word eventually found its way to Suzie's ear. Inevitably she *had a guy* who could help. Given what Faith knew about her mother, it was hard to believe that Suzie hadn't heard a whisper of something about the adoption.

"Wait until you have children of your own," Suzie continued. "Then you'll realize that with only so many hours in the day, something has to give. I guarantee it won't be your family."

Faith didn't fail to notice how adeptly her mother had shifted the subject. Nor did she fail to notice that Suzie hadn't really answered her question. Faith decided not to press. "I know we aren't having the get-married-and-have-kids discussion right now."

"Why not? You just went on a date with an interesting man, didn't you?"

"Yes. But it was only a first date. I'm certainly not going to start planning a future around him now."

"The way I hear it, you've been out with him already. Unless this is a different man you're talking about."

Faith sighed. "It's the same man. Which one of my sisters or cousins told you that?"

Suzie's laughter floated over the phone. "I never divulge my sources. You should know that by now."

Although Suzie couldn't see her, Faith nodded. One thing she'd always admired about her mother was her ability to keep a confidence. You could bare your soul to Suzie and never have to worry about hearing your words coming from someone else's lips. There were things that Faith had told her mother as a child that Suzie still kept to herself. Those things that no longer mattered to Faith were still sacred to Suzie.

"Fair enough. He's from Tenacity and wanted to see some of Bronco. So I obliged."

"You don't have to explain anything to me. You know I'm all for you meeting a man worthy of your love. Tenacity isn't as close to Bronco as I would like, but it's in this country. If you settle down with him, I'll see you more than I did last year."

"You're the one who raised me to be a free thinker and to follow my dreams."

Suzie chuckled. “I’m pretty sure that was your father.”

“I’m sure it was both of you, for which I will be forever grateful. The two of you raised strong women who know our own minds.” Faith’s father had been forced into an early retirement from the rodeo because of a leg injury, but he hadn’t become bitter. Instead, Arthur had devoted himself to making his daughters the best athletes—the best people—they could be.

“Being your own woman doesn’t mean you can’t have a family of your own,” Suzie said gently.

“I know. And believe me, when the right man comes along, I’ll welcome him with open arms.”

“How do you know you haven’t met him already?”

“Good question. One I’ll need to think about. Is it okay if I get back to you in say a year?”

Although she couldn’t see her mother, Faith knew Suzie was shaking her head. “I don’t think it will take that long, but okay.”

“On that note, I’m going to say good-night. As you pointed out, it’s way past my bedtime. Have a good night.”

“You too, my darling daughter.”

After ending the call, Faith closed her eyes and blew out a long breath, sad on Caleb’s behalf. She’d been so sure her mother would be able to help, so Suzie’s lack of knowledge was disappointing. Faith could ask her aunts. They’d been competing on the circuit thirty years ago too. But they’d been raising families back then as well. If Suzie didn’t know anything, Faith doubted her aunts would either.

But there was still her grandmother. Thirty years ago, Hattie hadn’t been performing as much as she had in her heyday, but she'd still been active in rodeo circles. Perhaps she would be able to help Caleb find the truth.

Faith didn't know why she was so determined to help him. They were barely friends. But his happiness mattered to her. One way or the other, she was going to help him find the answers he was looking for.

Chapter Seven

Caleb woke early the next morning, feeling quite happy. He was no closer to meeting with Brooks Langtree today than he had been yesterday. Nor had he come up with a new plan to make such a meeting a possibility. Given all of that, he should be discouraged. Despite the situation, he was grinning from ear to ear. It didn't take a genius to know why he was in such a good mood. It was all due to Faith Hawkins.

Just thinking about her made his already broad smile stretch even wider. Faith possessed a certain something that set her apart from everyone else. Something that made her special. Caleb was a simple man from a struggling Montana town yet somehow, he had managed to meet and capture the attention of this extraordinary woman. Any man in the world would be thrilled to spend time with Faith, yet she had chosen him. He wasn't going to question why. Instead he was going to thank his lucky stars and enjoy the ride for as long as it lasted.

He showered and dressed quickly. He was buttoning his shirt when his phone rang. He checked the screen and his smile returned, accompanied by a strong desire. *Faith.*

"I hope I didn't wake you," she said in that voice he was coming to love.

"Nope. I generally get up early. Most of our customers are ranchers, so we've got the store open before they start work."

"That's probably convenient for them. And good for business."

"Yes to both."

"Are you busy today?"

"No. I don't have any plans." That would have been disappointing before he'd met Faith. Now he was glad to be free.

"Good. I invited us to my grandmother's house for lunch."

"Don't tell me you're already trying to get me to meet the family?" he teased. "This when you wouldn't even kiss me last night. I don't think you understand how this dating thing works."

"Are we dating?"

"If you have to ask, then I guess not," he said dryly.

She laughed, a happy sound that touched his heart. "Maybe I was just seeking clarity."

"I'll accept that answer."

"So, are you interested in meeting my grandmother? You know, to talk to her about the hunt for your bio dad."

"You didn't mention this to her, did you?" Caleb managed to keep the panic from his voice, but just barely. He should have told Faith that he didn't want word getting out. He couldn't risk people guessing that he thought Brooks Langtree was his father when there was no proof. Brooks had to be the first person to learn about Caleb's suspicion.

"No. I figured you could tell her what you wanted her to know. But she knows everyone who was anyone in rodeo. She was also familiar with people who were just passing through. You know, the ones who liked the idea of being in rodeo more than the reality of constant travel and injuries."

"Then I would enjoy meeting her." Who knew what could come of that. Maybe Hattie Hawkins would be of some assistance. Even if she wasn't, he would be spending more time with Faith today.

"Hold on," Faith said. "That's her calling now."

As he waited, Caleb pictured Hattie Hawkins as she'd appeared on the stage during the Brooks Langtree Day ceremony. He guessed that she was in her early to middle seventies, although he couldn't be sure. She had that smooth skin that certain women had that defied age. From the easy way she moved, it was clear that she'd been an athlete in her younger days. Though he'd only seen them from a distance, Hattie and Brooks seemed to be enjoying each other's company. Maybe they were friends. If so, maybe she would know if Brooks had given up a child for adoption. Of course, he couldn't come out and ask her. That would raise too many questions he wasn't sure he could answer.

He was trying to come up with a way to broach the subject when Faith's voice came over the line. "That was Hattie. Something came up and she needs to reschedule. Do you mind?"

Disappointment threatened, but he shoved it down. Before Faith had called, he hadn't had an expectation of meeting with Hattie Hawkins. Nor had he even considered it was something he should do. Now he knew it was a possibility. If he had to wait a bit longer to talk to her, so be it. "That's fine by me."

"Good. Since I know you're free, do you still want to get together?"

"Are you asking me on a date, Ms. Hawkins?" he asked in a formal voice.

"I am indeed, Mr. Strom," Faith's replied, her tone mimicking his. "So, are you going to grace me with the pleasure of your company?"

"Absolutely. What did you have in mind?"

"I thought we could go apple picking. Unless that sounds too much like work."

He smiled. "We own a feed and farm supply store, so there is not much apple picking involved. Besides, a little physical activity is good for our health."

"I agree. I don't want to do too much sitting around. Being active keeps me in shape."

And what a good shape it was. "Then let's do it. It sounds like fun."

And not at all something he'd expected to interest Faith. Perhaps it was time for him to rid himself of his preconceived notions about her and relax and get to know her. She might be gorgeous, but she was also fun. Two qualities he found quite appealing. After setting a time for him to pick up Faith, Caleb called his parents and updated them on his progress or lack thereof. As usual, they were supportive and encouraged him to keep going. According to his mother, success was right around the corner. He might have agreed if he'd been able to meet with Hattie Hawkins.

He ordered some farm equipment that one of their customers had expressed an interest in, then reviewed online feed catalogues until it was time to head over to Faith's house. Although he had just seen her yesterday, and talked to her a few hours ago, he couldn't wait to see her again. There was no denying what was happening. He was falling for Faith. Hard. Given all that was going on in his life, that probably wasn't wise. He didn't need the distraction. But his heart rebelled at the idea of not seeing her again.

The drive to Faith's house was quick, and before long, he was ringing her doorbell. As he waited for her to answer the door, he looked up and down her block. The houses were of average size and each was well maintained, surrounded by trees ablaze with red, gold and orange leaves, proof that Fall had arrived in full force. Leaves were strewn on the sidewalk and scattered across the small, neat lawns. Two boys stood on opposite sides of the street, tossing a football back and forth. A young couple pedaled down the road on bicycles. They waved to him as they passed by. The entire scene felt optimistic.

He heard the locks disengage and turned around as the door swung open to reveal a smiling Faith. She was dressed in a tan and black print sweater, tight black jeans and tan cowboy boots. Her black hair was free around her shoulders, framing her face. Her bold red lipstick emphasized her irresistible, full lips. Her eyes sparkled with joy. Caleb felt his mouth gape open, but he was powerless to do anything other than stare. Faith was the sexiest woman he'd ever laid eyes on. She was petite, not even five foot three, but she was a dynamo with personality to spare.

Caleb had dated lots of women and not one made him laugh as much as Faith did. She managed to find the humor in every situation without making light of serious matters. And she was easy to talk to, open and candid. Just telling her about his search for his biological father had relieved some of his stress. He wasn't exactly relaxed about the situation, but he was no longer overwhelmed either.

Realizing that his mouth was still wide-open, he snapped it shut. "You look beautiful."

Faith smiled with pleasure. "Thank you. You don't look too shabby yourself."

"This old thing?" he asked, striking a pose.

"I like a man in faded jeans."

He liked her in everything. Caleb was positive he would *really* like her in his arms, and that he would *love* her in his bed. He shooed the thought away. There was no sense in getting ahead of himself. Especially when he wasn't in the position to maintain a relationship. "That's good to know. Especially since that describes a good portion of my wardrobe."

"Not mine. I have lots of clothes. You name the occasion and I have an outfit to wear."

"I like a woman who's prepared. No need for any last-minute shopping."

She put on her jacket and pulled her purse strap over her shoulder. "I didn't say that. Last-minute shopping is how I got such an extensive wardrobe."

As they drove to their destination, they talked about anything and everything under the sun.

"Turn at the corner and then head for the highway," Faith directed. "The pick-it-yourself orchard is about forty-five minutes from here."

He nodded. "Have you been apple picking before?"

"No. It just seemed like something fun. I like to keep myself open to new experiences. I don't want to fall into a rut, even doing things that I enjoy."

"You're adventurous. I like that about you."

"I don't know another way to be. If it sounds good, I'm willing to give it a try. What's the worst thing that could happen?"

He nodded. A sedan in front of them was traveling rather slowly, so Caleb passed it before looking back at Faith. "Does that adventurous nature ever get you into trouble?"

She hesitated a moment and then laughed. "More often than I care to admit. Although not as much lately. I remember when I was about fifteen and we were living in some small town. I don't remember which one exactly. It was a fall day and this girl who was my nemesis dared me to jump off of this ledge into a pond. This older boy we both liked was there with some of his friends. He was pretending not to be paying attention to us, but I could tell that he was."

Faith glanced over at Caleb and he nodded.

"Anyway, I couldn't let that dare stand. I've never enjoyed swimming all that much, especially in the cold water, but I rolled my eyes at her, adjusted my T-shirt and shorts, and then jumped in."

"It was a challenge so what else could you do?"

"I was in the middle of the air when my father's words telling me not to let my ego get me into trouble came back to me. He'd told me more than once that every adventure wasn't a good adventure. I hit the water and immediately began to sink. It was freezing and I gasped in a mouthful of water. I was struggling to get back to the surface when out of nowhere these strong arms grabbed me."

"The boy you liked?" Caleb guessed.

"Yep. Now, I could swim mind you. My parents started me in lessons at the Y when I was three. But I figured I should let him play the hero."

He laughed. "I'm sure he appreciated it."

"Of course, it wasn't all pretense. Flying through the air was the scariest hour of my life and I felt weak."

"Hour? I don't know how high that ledge was, but I doubt it was longer than a second or two."

Faith flashed a cheeky grin. "Time stretches when you're terrified."

"I'll have to take your word for it."

She shook her head. "You are such a guy. Of course you've never been terrified."

"Not that I'll admit to. So what happened next?"

"The guy, whose name I can't remember, invited me to sit around the bonfire with him and his friends so my clothes could dry and I could get warm. My nemesis watched on with envy. I would have laughed in her face if I hadn't been shaking so badly."

"I guess no big romance resulted since you can't even remember the guy's name."

"No. After spending an hour or so with him and his friends, I discovered that he was kind of a jerk, so I invited my nemesis to join us." She chuckled at the memory.

"One jerk deserves another?"

"Yep." Faith sobered. "But I decided that moment that being adventurous was not the same as being reckless. I made up my mind not to be so willing to try everything. At least not for the wrong reasons. I've had more fun since then."

"I bet you were a handful growing up."

Faith's beautiful smile returned. "I refuse to answer that on the grounds that it might incriminate me."

"Yeah. I got my answer."

"Enough about me. What about you?" She gave him an assessing look and he wondered just how he came across to her. Would he appeal to her or would she find him to be boring? After all, his life experiences didn't compare to hers.

"What about me?"

"What kind of kid were you?"

He smiled. "I was a good kid. A rule follower. I didn't get into much trouble."

She nodded slowly. "I can see that about you. Don't worry. Stick with me. I'm sure I can find some mischief for us to get into. That is if you're game."

"I'm not a kid any longer. I'm sure I'll be more than up for whatever you come up with. The question is, will you be daring enough to do whatever I come up with?"

She gave him a look hot enough to melt steel. "I guess you'll have to wait and see."

That was all right with him. He just hoped there wasn't a lot of waiting before they got around to the seeing part.

They talked about other things until they spotted a sign for the apple orchard. There were numerous arrows directing them, so he found the parking lot rather easily. They climbed from his vehicle and walked through the lot and to the entrance. Bushel baskets were stacked inside and they each grabbed one. A teenager wearing earbuds and clearly not interested in conversation handed them each a map before looking back down at his phone.

Caleb and Faith exchanged glances before walking away.

"I so recognize that age," Faith said.

"Me too. I bet that he's the owner's son and has no choice but to work here."

"Did you act that way when working for your dad?"

"As a teenager? Yep. I wanted to be somewhere where I could meet girls. Believe it or not, they didn't frequent the feedstore."

"I know that. I am a girl, remember?"

He looked her up and down, taking note of her sexy body. Even dressed casually, she was the most gorgeous woman he had ever seen. "I don't think I could ever forget that."

She smiled and then, clearly flustered, she looked down at her map. "They have a couple of different types of apples growing here. Which type do you want?"

"It doesn't matter to me. I'll eat whatever kind you want."

"Honey crisp it is."

There were lots of people walking about, taking advantage of the nice fall weather. Faith and Caleb found several trees in a secluded area near the edge of the orchard. A step ladder was leaning against the trunk of each tree and they each grabbed one.

Caleb glanced over at Faith who grinned at him. Her smile was so bright, so open, that he couldn't look away from her to save his life. There was a vibrancy to her that struck him to his core. He could get used to having her in his life. Of course, until he settled the issue of his father, he would have to put that interest on the backburner.

He stood by her as she climbed onto the lowest rung. They were eye level and her luscious lips were tantalizingly close. It would be so easy to lean in and kiss her. Before he could decide whether that was a good idea or one he should ignore, she poked him in the shoulder with a perfectly manicured nail.

Her eyes danced with mischief. "I'm not going to fall so I don't need you to stand guard over me."

"How do I know you're not scare of heights?"

"I'm not. Are you?"

"What do you think?" He stepped onto the bottom rung of his ladder and then looked down at her.

"I think I liked it better when we were the same height."

So did he.

They picked apples in silence for a while, but he didn't feel the need to fill the space. There was a connection developing between them that didn't need conversation in order to remain intact. Besides, he liked the quiet. It was comfortable and relaxing in a way that he hadn't experienced before with another woman.

The day was perfect with a clear, blue sky. Every once in a while a cool breeze blew, filling the air with the scent of dry grass and leaves.

After a while, Faith stepped off her ladder and used the rung as a seat.

"Finished?" he asked, coming to stand beside her.

"Yes." She looked into her nearly filled basket and then over at his. He'd climbed up and down the ladder more quickly than she had and his basket was full. "What are you going to do with all of those apples?"

"Good question." He hadn't thought that far ahead. In fact, he hadn't thought about it at all. He'd simply been enjoying himself and the beautiful day. Now he rubbed the back of his neck and looked up at the sky as if searching for inspiration. "What are you going to do with yours?"

"My horse likes apples. So do my sisters' and cousins'. I suppose I could give the ones I don't eat to them."

"I don't suppose you would be interested in baking a pie or two?"

"Do you mean *with* you or *for* you?"

"Whatever answer will get me a pie."

She laughed. "With you."

They leaned their ladders back against the tree trunk, grabbed their baskets and headed for the exit. After paying for the apples, they loaded the fruit into his vehicle and he drove back to her house.

Once they were in her kitchen she leaned against the counter and smiled sheepishly. "I suppose we've reached the part of the program where I confess that I have never baked an apple pie from scratch in my life. Or any pie for that matter."

He threw his head back and laughed. "What about all that big talk you spouted about making cookies so good I would lose my mind after just one taste?"

"I stand by what I said. But cookies and pies are two different things. Surely you know that."

"I do. Lucky for you, I can make apple pie."

The look of surprise on her face was one he would

never forget. It was quickly replaced by sheer joy. "Really?"

He nodded. "I love apple pie, so my mother insisted that I learn how to bake them for myself. That way I can have a pie whenever I want."

"For the record, I love your mother."

"So do I. Now let's get to work. I'm getting hungry."

The first time Caleb had baked an apple pie, he'd been with his mother. She'd been a patient teacher and he'd enjoyed himself. Once he'd mastered the task, he'd made pies on his own.

Neither of those experiences compared to working in the kitchen with Faith. She took things to a whole different level. She'd turned on some music and bobbed her head as she peeled apples. When a popular song came on, she set the apple into the bowl and used her knife as a microphone, singing gustily and shaking her hips to the beat.

Caleb put down his knife, leaned against the counter, and watched with amusement mixed with a hint of lust.

"Don't tell me you don't know this song," Faith said.

"Of course I do. It only comes on the radio every hour if not more."

"Then grab a mic," she said. "I could use a backup singer."

Grabbing his knife, he went and stood behind Faith and began to blast out the background vocals. His eyes strayed to her round bottom as she danced and he admitted it was a pleasurable sight to see.

She turned and caught him staring. The uptempo song ended and a ballad began to play. Setting down her knife, she held out her hands to him. Without hesitating, he dropped his knife on the counter and took her into his arms. As they slow danced, her sweet scent floated around him. She fit perfectly in his arms and he closed his eyes, enjoying the feel of her soft body pressed up against him.

The urge to kiss her was strong, but he wouldn't act on it. He wasn't in the position to offer her a relationship. When the song ended, he forced himself to release her and get back to the work.

Once the pie was baking, they put together a quick dinner and then sat at the table to eat. The kitchen was small and Caleb appreciated the intimacy. Though he'd enjoyed their time at the apple orchard earlier, nothing felt as good as being alone with her.

They ate in silence for a couple of minutes. Then Faith looked at him. "You've seen my town. Now tell me about yours. What is it like?"

"Different from Bronco."

Faith scoffed. "That's like saying it's different from Chicago or Paris. It tells me absolutely nothing."

"Okay. Before I answer, tell me this. Are you still in touch with your friends from high school?"

"Yes. A couple of them. Why?"

"I've done a lot of walking around Bronco over these past couple of days. I've seen lots of young people here. Couples in their twenties are settling down and starting families. People are starting careers and opening businesses."

"Yes."

"That's not happening in Tenacity. I don't think a single member of my high school graduating class still lives there."

"Really? Are you serious?"

"That might be a bit of an exaggeration, but not by much. There aren't many opportunities there, so once kids graduate they move and don't come back. My parents insisted that I get my college degree, so I went away to Howard University. When I came back I didn't see many familiar faces. I didn't see any new ones either. The kids I used to hang out with on Friday and Saturday nights had packed up and moved in search of greener pastures. I joined the family business. We hire as many local people as we can, but there's only so much a small business like ours can do."

"Wow."

"I know we're only a hundred or so miles apart, but the differences between Tenacity and Bronco are stark. We've had some bad financial luck in town for well over a decade or so, and nobody in town seems to know how to reverse the trend. But the mayor and the city council are trying to attract younger people and more businesses."

"Surely there must be something good happening there."

He thought for a moment. "Well, we have the Tenacity Winter Holiday Pageant."

"What's that?"

"It's a holiday program. Last year the choir's multicultural presentation went viral."

"Cool."

"We all thought so."

"Do you plan to stay there or are you going to join the exodus?"

"I'm staying," Caleb replied instantly. "I love Tenacity. Despite all of its flaws and its current state, it's home.

Besides, I'm not the type to abandon ship simply because the waters are a bit rough. I know there's a way to turn things around, and I plan to be a part of it."

Faith smiled and held up her glass in toast. "Here's to the future being even better than the past. I hope you get everything you want."

So did he. And suddenly Faith Hawkins was at the top of that list.

Chapter Eight

"I'm sorry that I had to cancel our meeting yesterday," Hattie said as she held out a hand to Faith, welcoming her into her home. Hattie had moved to Bronco a year or so ago, but her house was filled with items that gave the comfortable home a familiar feeling. Faith had learned over the years that it wasn't the building that made a home. Or even the furnishings. It was the family that lived there. The love that they shared. Whether she'd been on the road with her parents, sleeping in a hotel room in some small town off the highway, or in her bed at home, it was the love that made her feel secure in the knowledge that she belonged. Bronco was home now, but she knew any place in the world would feel the same as long as people she loved were there.

"I understand," Faith said. "I just hope you can help me out."

"I will if I can. Would you like a drink?"

"Yes."

"So, will your friend be joining us, or will it be just the two of us?"

"Just us."

Caleb had returned home to Tenacity early that morning, as planned. Even though his father had claimed to have everything under control at the store, Caleb had insisted on going back to work. He was an active partner and wanted to pull his weight. Faith appreciated how responsible he was even though she'd hated watching him drive off.

"Well, maybe next time."

Faith nodded and followed Hattie into the kitchen. Her grandmother always made everything special. While others might nuke a cup of water, dunk in a tea bag and call it a day, Hattie used a teapot and loose leaves. And she also always had cookies to go with it. It was a production that always made Faith feel valued. As a little girl, tea with Hattie had always made her feel grown-up and sophisticated.

Hattie filled the kettle and then set the water to boil. She withdrew several homemade cookies from an old-fashioned, bear-shaped ceramic cookie jar and put them on a plate. Faith grabbed napkins from a drawer that held the kitchen linen and set them on the coffee table in the living room. Hattie soon followed behind, pushing a cart with the porcelain tea set on it through the narrow room. She poured tea into two delicate, gold-rimmed cups, handed one to Faith and kept the other for herself.

"Help yourself to some cookies."

Faith grinned as she placed two maple cookies on a delicate saucer. These had always been her favorites. Knowing that Hattie had baked them especially for her made them taste twice as good. "Thank you."

As they sipped their tea, they chatted about recent events.

"So, what is this favor?" Hattie asked, setting her empty cup on the table.

Faith swallowed her bite of cookie and dabbed her mouth with her napkin before answering. "It's for a friend. He was given up for adoption thirty years ago and knows very little about his birth family. He believes that his father was in the rodeo back then. I asked Mom, but she doesn't have a clue."

"Really?" Hattie's eyebrows disappeared beneath her salt-and-pepper bangs. "That doesn't sound like Suzie."

"I didn't think so either. But she said she'd just adopted me and she was busy with her family."

"I suppose…" Hattie said, but she didn't sound totally convinced. "Well, anyway, what do you need from me?"

"Do you remember hearing anything about that?"

"No." Hattie pursed her lips and slowly shook her head. "It's possible that his father didn't have a connection to the rodeo at all. He might have been a local laborer who helped out while the rodeo was in town. Many people did that."

Faith shook her head. "He's certain that his father was part of the rodeo. He didn't tell me why and I didn't want to pry."

"I understand. The man is entitled to his secrets." Hattie folded her hands in her lap and closed her eyes, thinking. Then she opened them again and looked at Faith. "My memory isn't what it used to be, so nothing comes to mind."

Faith sighed. Though she'd been disappointed when her grandmother canceled the initial meeting with Caleb, now she was glad that he wasn't here to hear what her grandmother had to say. Her stomach churned with regret for getting his hopes up when she didn't have any answers for him. Next time she would keep any information she received to herself, until she had something solid.

"Thanks anyway."

"Don't be so glum, Faith. I might not remember details right now, but I've collected lots of souvenir programs, pictures and newspaper clippings from over the years. I can go through my trunk and see what I have from thirty years ago. That might refresh my memory."

"I hope it's not too much trouble."

"It's no trouble at all. I'll take any excuse I can get to take a trip down memory lane." She tapped a manicured fingernail against her forehead. "This is filled with wonderful memories."

"In that case, I'm glad to be of service."

They laughed together. Hattie refilled their cups and then they reminisced about happy times they'd shared together, laughing and talking long after the last of the tea and cookies were gone.

After a while, Faith stood. "I suppose I need to get going. Let me help you with the dishes."

Hattie swatted aside Faith's hands. She had a certain way of washing and putting away her tea service. "You know I have it covered."

"I do. But Mom would have a fit if I didn't at least offer."

"I'll be sure to let her know that the lessons in manners took."

Faith laughed because she knew her grandmother would do just that. Whenever the grandchildren spent time with Hattie, she'd always given a report to their parents. Of course, she'd always edited out misbehavior, claiming it was not worth mentioning.

"It's always good to see you," Hattie said later as they walked to the door. Faith carried a plastic container with a half dozen cookies inside.

"Same." They embraced before Faith left, her spirits high with expectation. Perhaps her grandmother could turn up valuable information after all. Hopefully, she would have something good to tell Caleb soon. She was looking forward to the day when he came back.

Faith put her desire to see Caleb on the back burner as she drove to the stables. She wasn't scheduled to appear in a rodeo for another couple of weeks, but she liked to keep her skills sharp. Several of her family members also boarded their horses at the same stables, and if she was lucky, one or more of them would be there too. It would be good to have someone else to talk to about Caleb. It was one thing to talk to her mother and grandmother about him, but as open-minded as they were, she doubted that either of them would be comfortable listening to Faith lust after him. Not to mention that she wouldn't feel comfortable talking about it either.

Imagining that conversation, Faith laughed out loud as she got out of the car.

"What's so funny?"

Faith turned as her cousins Corinne and Remi and her sister Amy approached her. Corinne and Remi competed as the Hawkins Sisters here in the United States with their sisters Audrey and Brynn. The two often competed together in team events. Faith grinned. "I was just imagining telling grandma and my mother about a guy

I like. Can you picture their faces as I talked about his cute butt?"

"The guy from Brooks Langtree Day?" Corinne asked.

"How do you even know about that? You weren't there."

"Surely you weren't in South America long enough to forget how things work around here. If one Hawkins woman knows something in the morning, we all know by noon."

Faith laughed. "Oh, no."

"Caleb isn't supposed to be a secret, is he?" Amy asked, and Faith wondered if she'd located the source of the information.

"No. In fact I was hoping that I would run into someone to talk to about him."

"Lucky for you, you've run into three of us," Corinne said. "I'm sure everyone is tired of hearing me talk about Mike."

"I'm not," Faith said. "I would love to hear more about your fiancé, the future doctor."

Corinne smiled. "We can talk about him later."

"For the record, I'm not tired of listening to you talk about Mike either," Remi said, proving why she was a favorite of all the cousins. She was loyal to a fault and sweet as pie.

"That's good to know," Corinne said. The two linked arms as they walked toward the stables. "And I'm going to take you up on that very soon. Right now I want to hear all about Faith's new man."

"Fair enough," Remi said, looking at Faith. "It's decided. We're going to talk about your guy first. Then we can talk about Amy and Tru McCoy."

Faith stopped walking and turned to look at her sister. "Tru McCoy? The actor? Why am I just now hearing about this? What happened to the Hawkins Sisters telling each other everything?"

Amy held up her hands, stopping Faith before she could ask her any more questions. "I'll tell you the same thing I told Corinne and Remi. There is nothing to tell."

"But you were talking to him at the Golden Buckle Rodeo. Remi and I saw the two of you together."

"Only for a minute. It was nothing," Amy insisted, her eyes darting around, never meeting any of them in the eyes. "So let's change the subject."

Faith exchanged glances with Remi and Corinne. Neither of them believed Amy's denial. It was clear that she was holding something back. But they all loved and respected her too much to push, especially when she was clearly uncomfortable.

"Okay," Remi said. "Let's get back to talking about Faith's boyfriend."

"Whoa. You're a few steps ahead of me," Faith said. "I wouldn't exactly call Caleb my boyfriend."

"Call him whatever you want as long as you tell us all about him," Corinne said, a mischievous grin on her face. "I want to know everything. Don't leave out a single detail."

"Don't worry. I won't," Faith said and then laughed. "I love having a willing audience even though there isn't that much to share."

Their horses were housed in stalls in the same aisle. The grooms took excellent care of them, but the Hawkins women had been raised to be responsible for their own horses. The horses were their partners and were treated as such. The four women checked the animals' hooves and brushed them before saddling them and leading them into the corral. Once the women were all in the saddle they let their horses trot. As they rode, Faith told them about Caleb.

"He sounds like a good guy," Corinne said when Faith concluded. "A kind guy."

"A hot guy," Remi said. "He wouldn't by chance have a brother, would he? I haven't been able to find a good man on my own."

Faith shook her head. She intentionally hadn't brought up Caleb's search for his birth father. For all she knew, he might have another sibling out there somewhere. But she wasn't going to speculate. She was going to stick with the information that he had provided her. "He's an only child."

"Darn. How about a cousin? Or maybe even a young uncle?" Remi said, chuckling.

"Not that she's desperate or anything," Amy said with a grin.

"Not at all," Remi said. "I'm just expanding my search parameters."

They laughed together before Faith sobered. "I don't know anything about that."

"If the opportunity arises, feel free to ask on my behalf." Remi winked.

"I'll be sure of it."

They teased Remi for a few minutes more before they got down to work, putting their horses through the paces. When they were finished, they led their horses back to their respective stalls. After removing their saddles and blankets, they brushed their horses and inspected their hooves. After checking their water and food, the cousins left the stable.

"It was good to see you guys," Faith said as they walked back to their cars. "We need to have a cousins night out soon."

"Agreed. Now that you and most of your sisters are back in the States we should get together at least once a month," Remi said.

"I'll tell Tori and Elizabeth if you guys tell Audrey and Brynn," Amy volunteered. "Maybe we can all get together in the next couple of weeks."

"That sounds like a plan," Corinne said.

Faith climbed into her car while Amy and her cousins walked to theirs. Today had been nice, but now that she was alone, she was thinking of Caleb. She missed him and her heart ached to see him again.

And that was a problem.

Caleb sat down at the dinner table in the same chair he'd used every night from the time he was a child until he'd moved out a few years ago. The familiarity felt good, especially considering everything else that was going on in his life. He and his parents usually ate dinner together on Sunday nights, but since he'd been in Bronco last week, he'd been unable to come. He and Faith had made plans to spend this weekend together, so he wouldn't be around this upcoming Sunday either, so he made sure to be here for dinner tonight. Now, of all time, he didn't want to do anything to make his parents feel neglected. He was very careful to make sure they knew just how important they were to him.

"It's been good to have you home," Iris said, setting

the green beans on the table beside the pot roast, mashed potatoes and rolls.

"It's good to be back." Instead of a typical Thursday night meal, his mother had gone all out. There was a chocolate cake sitting on the kitchen counter, waiting to be served with the homemade vanilla ice cream.

Nathan held Iris's chair for her before taking his own. Once they were all served, they talked about the goings-on in town. Eventually the conversation turned to his search for Caleb's biological father. Not that there was anything new to tell. He still hadn't met the man. Despite his best efforts to remain positive, doubt was beginning to creep in. Maybe he'd gotten as close to Brooks Langtree as he was ever going to get.

"So, what do you plan to do?" his mother asked when he'd finished with his recap.

"Faith thinks that she has a way to help. She's asked her mother but the woman didn't know anything. She's going to ask her grandmother next. Hopefully, she'll be able to help. I guess I'll find out when I get back."

He and Faith had talked on the phone several times this past week, but he hadn't wanted to talk about his search. He wanted their relationship to be about more than that.

"And if things are still at a standstill?" Nathan's question hung in the air for a moment.

"What do you mean?"

"Will you stay in Bronco so you can spend more time with Faith?"

"Don't matchmake," Iris said. "Caleb is quite capable of finding a good woman without your encouragement.

He knows how much we want grandchildren to spend the weekends with us before we get too old."

Caleb smiled at how slickly Iris chastised Nathan while simultaneously mentioning her desire for grandchildren.

"I wasn't thinking about grandchildren spending the weekend with us," Nathan denied. "I like having my best girl all to myself."

"Oh, you," Iris said, smiling like a teenager.

Caleb watched the interaction between his parents. They hadn't changed a bit in thirty years. His father was romantic and flirtatious while his mother was more reserved. They were the perfect couple. Caleb wondered if he would ever find his perfect mate. *Perhaps you've found her in Faith.* The thought, although appealing, wasn't appropriate right now and he refocused on the conversation.

"I'll stay the weekend either way. As you pointed out more than once, finding my birth father might take a while. I'm in it for the long haul."

"You might have a bit more success if you actually told the man what you believe. If he's not your biological father, you'll know and be able to continue your search elsewhere."

"That's my plan. But I want to tell him and *only* him. If I'm wrong, I don't want to be the source of gossip that might reach his family and friends. And I definitely don't want it to reach the media who might run with it. Especially after all of the accolades that he just received."

Iris patted his hand. "You always were a good and considerate child. You're an even better man."

Caleb's heart warmed at his mother's praise. "Thank you."

"When are you leaving?"

"I figured I'd leave tomorrow afternoon. Faith and I have plans to spend the evening together."

Iris smiled and patted Nathan's hand. "It looks like we might be getting those grandkids after all."

"Don't get ahead of yourself, Mom," Caleb said, rolling his eyes. "One thing at a time. We're still getting to know each other. Besides, with everything that's going on, I don't have time for a serious relationship."

Iris only nodded and Caleb knew that she was going to think whatever she pleased. Surprisingly he wasn't annoyed. In fact, he liked the idea of Faith having a more permanent role in his life. But first, he needed to know whether Brooks Langtree was his biological father. Until he knew that, romance was off the table.

Chapter Nine

"How do you feel about Halloween?" Faith asked Friday night as she and Caleb walked around the Bronco Fairgrounds, taking in the sights. They'd spent the past few hours enjoying the Bronco Harvest Festival. They'd played a few games, winning a few strings of beads, and gone on a hayride. It was slightly chilly, but nothing their cups of warm cider couldn't chase away. There was a stray piece of hay clinging to the front of her sweater and she brushed it off.

Caleb shrugged and Faith's eyes were immediately drawn to his massive shoulders. "I don't feel any kind of way. We always give out candy at the store and at home. Other than that, it's just a normal day."

"Do you wear a costume?"

"I haven't since I was a kid."

"But you aren't opposed to dressing up, are you?" she asked, mentally crossing her fingers.

Caleb stepped in front of Faith, stopping her progress. A kid holding a pink cotton candy nearly ran into him, veering away at the last minute. "I get the feeling there's something behind these questions. Why don't you just get to the point?"

"I want to invite you to a Halloween party."

"With costumes?"

She nodded.

"Sure. It might be fun."

"Great. I was hoping you would say that. It's tomorrow."

"*Tomorrow?* Tomorrow isn't Halloween. In fact, Halloween isn't for weeks. That is if we're talking about the same Halloween that we observe in Tenacity and the rest of the country."

"Ha ha. You're cute."

He puffed out his chest and struck a model pose. "Think so? My mother always says I'm her most handsome son. But then, I'm an only child, so…" He gave a half smile.

"You don't fool me for a minute. I bet the women in Tenacity are falling all over themselves to get to you."

He actually looked embarrassed. *Was he blushing?* "I do all right."

She laughed. It was good to know he wasn't vain.

"If we're comparing looks, you're going to win by a mile, Faith. You're more than cute."

Her heart skipped a beat and she struggled to calm down. She didn't want to let herself be led astray by one comment, so she forced herself to get back on track and started walking again. "Back to the party. It's more of a pre-Halloween party if you want to get technical. But there will be costumes and decorations."

"Is there a reason for the early date?"

"Yes." She held back a grin.

"Are you going to share that with me or is it a state

secret? You know, you'd tell me but then you'd have to kill me."

She laughed. "It's the last day of the Bronco Harvest Festival. The organizers decided to have a costume party to cap off the event. Why? Are you a purist? Are you philosophically opposed to attending a Halloween party on any day but October thirty-first?"

He snorted. "A purist? No, I'm not."

"Then you'll go to the party with me tomorrow?" She held her breath as she waited for his response. When she realized what she was doing, she exhaled forcefully. There was no need to make this a bigger deal than it was.

"Sure. But I don't have a costume. Or are costumes optional in this newfangled Halloween party?"

"I don't think that costumes are required but wearing them will make the party a lot more fun."

"What are you going as?"

"I don't know. I don't have a costume yet." She hadn't even planned on going until Caleb had come into her life.

"I have an idea. You can go as a rodeo star and I can go as the owner of a feed and farm supply store." His dimples flashed in his cheeks and she held back a smile.

"I'm going to pretend that you didn't say that. I don't wear work clothes to a party."

"Then what are we going to do for costumes? There's not much time."

"We're going to make them."

"You mean like sewing? Because if that's what you have in mind, I need to warn you that I'm useless with a needle and thread."

"For shame. I can sew. But that's not what I had in mind. There are some great shops in town where we can buy some vintage clothing and create our own costumes. I heard there'll be prizes for best costume and most original. Things like that. If we make our own as opposed to getting one at a store, we'll have a better chance of winning."

"And winning matters?" Caleb looked at her, a question in his eyes.

She shrugged. "It doesn't hurt. Besides it'll be fun to get our pictures taken with one of the trophies. You'll see."

She stopped and looked into his eyes. They were still a bit wary but he appeared to be warming up to the idea. So she continued. "Here's the plan. Tomorrow morning we'll hit some vintage clothing shops. If we don't find what we need there, we'll branch out. We can get any other supplies we need at the hardware store." She was winging it, but the more she thought about it, the more exciting the prospect became.

"So I guess we won't be cutting eyeholes in sheets and going as ghosts," Caleb quipped.

"Ghosts are invisible. Everybody knows that."

"Really? I must have been absent from school the day they taught that."

"Good thing you met me."

He grinned slowly. "Yes, Faith, it is."

Her stomach fluttered and she made herself ignore the feeling. "Anyway, we need to come up with something original."

"Hmm. I do like a challenge. I like the rodeo theme. But maybe with a twist. Instead of going as a horse, we could go as a camel. Our heads will be the humps."

Despite herself, Faith laughed. “What do camels have to do with rodeo?”

“Good point. But remember I’m a rodeo novice.”

“Clearly.”

“How about two peas in a pod?” Caleb said. He looked serious for a good three seconds before he burst into laughter. *Thank goodness.*

“I’m glad that you’re getting into the spirit of things,” she said with a wry smile.

“Totally. Maybe we could go as two pieces of bread. Heck, we could ask one of your sisters to join us and go as a sandwich.”

Faith laughed. “Now you’re just being silly.”

He came up with one outrageous suggestion after the other, making her laugh uproariously, which drew the attention of several passersby.

Faith’s sides were aching from laughter by the time Caleb finally ran out of suggestions.

“Do you want to eat breakfast together tomorrow before we hit the stores?” she asked.

“Absolutely. We can’t start Operation Costumes on an empty stomach.” Caleb stepped closer and whispered. “Should we synchronize our watches? Maybe have a secret code word in case anyone is looking?”

“I don’t wear a watch. Not to mention the clocks on our phones are synchronized. But a code word is a good idea. What do you have in mind?”

His eyes widened in surprise. “You’re kidding, right?”

“That’s kind of long, but I suppose it’ll work in a pinch.”

Caleb shook his head. “You know, I like you, Faith Hawkins. I like you a lot.”

And just like that, the playfulness fled and was replaced by a warm sensation. His sincerely spoken words were exactly what she'd longed to hear. At the same time, it was exactly what she was afraid of hearing. The emotions he awakened in her were strong. She hadn't felt anything like them before, yet they felt oddly familiar. They were simultaneously comforting and terrifying. But she knew she had nothing to fear from Caleb. She might not have known him for long but she knew he was a good man. A man she could trust.

"I like you too, Caleb." They'd stopped walking and were now facing each other, standing so close that she could feel the warmth from his body reaching out and surrounding hers. With each breath she took, she inhaled his enticing, masculine scent. She tried to fight back a sigh but it escaped her lips.

Caleb reached out and caressed her face. His touch was gentle and she leaned into his palm. "So, Faith, is the no-kissing rule still in effect?"

"No. It actually expired that night."

"That's good to know." His voice was a hoarse whisper that sent chills racing down her spine.

Her heart pounded in anticipation. "So, what are you going to do about it?"

Rather than answer, he leaned over and brushed his lips against hers. Her lips began to tingle and heat blossomed in her stomach before flowing throughout her body. Her eyes drifted shut. After a few seconds, he moved away, ending the kiss.

Opening her eyes, she looked at him, not bothering to disguise her frustration. A self-satisfied expression was written on his face. Clearly he knew that she was expecting more than that simple kiss. She poked him in his chest, absently noting just how hard and muscular it was. He laughed.

"What did you expect?" he asked. "We're in the middle of the Festival. Kids are running around and I don't want somebody's parents giving me the evil eye. And don't forget that every phone is a camera. I didn't think you would appreciate being the topic of conversation for the next couple of days and possibly even going viral."

"I don't care about that. I'm a Hawkins Sister. People are always talking about one of us."

"And that doesn't bother you?"

She gave a one-shoulder shrug. "If you can't stand the attention, don't compete in rodeo."

"So you wouldn't mind people talking about you making out in public with some strange—although incredibly handsome—man? You wouldn't care if that gossip reached your parents and grandmother?"

"I didn't say that. Besides, we weren't exactly making out."

"Not yet." Grinning mischievously, he reached for her. "But there's nothing stopping us."

She dodged his grasp. Turnabout was fair play. "It's too late now. The mood has passed."

He dropped his hand and his grin fell away. "That was fast."

"As my grandmother likes to say, you snooze, you lose."

"I wasn't exactly napping. But now I know I have to move fast with you."

"Sometimes and in some ways. Other times, slow is better. I'll leave it to you to determine which is which."

She realized just how suggestive that comment was, but she didn't take it back. There was no sense denying the sexual attraction between them. The only question was how long it would simmer before it boiled over.

He nodded slowly. Then without saying a word, he grabbed her hand and they began walking across the fairgrounds again. His firm palm pressed against hers felt heavenly. She could get used to this.

Caleb's heart began to race as he walked beside Faith to her front door. It had taken all of his self-control to limit himself to a brief kiss earlier. The feel of her soft lips had sent his imagination into overdrive and he'd yearned to pull her into his arms and deepen the kiss. But his common sense had overruled his urges. Faith might not mind being the subject of gossip, but he did. He preferred to keep some things private. Especially since he might be the long-lost son of a big rodeo star. Caleb didn't want anything he did to sully Brooks Langtree's pristine reputation. If they were related, Brooks would come under scrutiny for everything that Caleb did, so he had to be sure not to step out of line.

But that was a worry for another time. Caleb and Faith were no longer standing in the middle of a busy festival. They were alone on her secluded porch and not another soul was around. The mature trees blocked out a great deal of the moonlight, casting romantic shadows that shifted as the wind blew. The smell of smoke from a neighbor's fireplace filled the crisp autumn air.

Faith leaned against her front door and looked up at him. There was a gleam in her eyes that made his pulse race. She placed a hand on his chest and his heart began to pound. A small fire ignited inside him. His desire for her grew by each passing second and his control began to weaken.

She leaned closer, her sweet scent teasing his senses. "Just in case you need a hint, this is where I would like you to make a move."

"Is that right?" He placed his hands on her waist and pulled her closer to him. Her soft body molded against his, and his desire nearly consumed him. And yet he prolonged the moment, tormenting both of them. "I think I can handle that."

Ever so slowly, he lowered his head, drawing out the moment until the sexual tension between them fairly sizzled. Then their lips met. Instantly the fire inside him blazed hotter and intense desire spread from his head to his toes. He wrapped his arms around her, pulling her small, soft body even closer to his.

Caleb licked the seam of Faith's lips and she opened her mouth to him. Immediately he swept inside and their tongues tangled and danced. She tasted sweet and hot and his desire threatened to overwhelm his good sense. Caleb knew he should slow things down, but his body wouldn't let him. Instead, he deepened the kiss, indulging the pleasure he'd waited all day to feel.

Way too soon, he felt Faith easing back from him. Though his mind was hazy with lust, he understood her message and immediately loosened his hold on her, ending the kiss. Instead of backing away as he'd expected, Faith leaned her head against his chest. He was breathing hard, inhaling big gulps of air as he sought to catch his breath. He was vaguely aware of Faith doing the same. After a moment, she took a step back. Instantly Caleb missed the physical connection. He longed to reach out and pull her back to him but he resisted.

"Wow." Her quivering voice was filled with wonder.

"You took the word right out of my mouth." His voice sounded hoarse to his ears and he cleared his throat. A part of him wanted to continue this inside and see where things might go, but he shoved that thought aside. Faith had made herself clear and he respected her right to end things here. Besides, he was in the middle of searching for his birth father. He didn't know where that would take him. For all he knew, he might not be in Montana next week. He didn't want to start something with Faith he might not be able to finish. She deserved someone who could give her all of his attention. Someone who could promise to always be here for her. If things were different, he would pursue her in a heartbeat. But until he found his birth father, there would be no woman in his life.

"I suppose I should go in now." Faith's voice was reluctant and she didn't move.

He brushed a strand of her hair away from her face, letting his fingers skim over the soft, warm skin of her cheek. It wouldn't take much for him to get her aroused again, but he wouldn't. He took a step back and shoved his fist into his pocket to keep from reaching out to her again.

Faith pulled her keys from her purse, fumbling with the ring. She sorted through the keys until she found the right one. She held one and aimed it for the lock. And missed. Caleb covered her hand with his, steered the key into the lock, then turned the knob. Faith pushed open the door and looked back at him. Her eyes were dark and dreamy and his earlier resolve threatened to crumble.

"Thank you for a good day, Caleb. I had a wonderful time."

"So did I."

"I'll see you in the morning."

"Yes." Nothing would keep him away.

She raised on tiptoes and brushed a kiss on his lips. She lingered for a moment and then broke the contact. His lips were still tingling when she stepped inside and closed the door behind her. He leaned his head against the frame for a moment before turning and jogging down the stairs, hoping the brisk night air would cool him off.

Tonight had been great. Tomorrow promised to be even better. He couldn't wait.

Chapter Ten

"Bacon and eggs? Really?" Faith pressed her lips together as she struggled to hold in her laughter. It slipped out anyway. She placed a hand on her hip. They were in the middle of a secondhand shop trying to find something to make their costumes with. They'd already hit a couple of stores in town but hadn't met with success. "What is it with you and food costumes?"

Caleb held up the pants in front of him and looked at her. He dragged his hand over the various shades of brown wavy stripes. "You cannot tell me that these pants don't look like slices of bacon."

He had a point, but she wasn't going to tell him that. That would only encourage him to make more outrageous costume suggestions. Not that she minded much. Caleb was a one-man comedy show. She couldn't remember the last time she'd laughed this hard or as much. But time was slipping by and they needed to find a costume. "I'm not going to answer. We have work to do."

Caleb hung the pants back on the rack. Then he smiled. "Be right back. I see something."

"That sounds ominous," Faith said, following him across the store.

"You aren't the only one who will know it when you see it," Caleb said, echoing the words she'd said earlier.

She still believed them to be true. But she needed to see *"it"* soon. "So you say."

Caleb grabbed a hanger from a rack and then whipped it around with a flourish. He smiled confidently at her. "Great, huh?"

She looked at the yards of dark blue velvet fabric in his hands. "What is it supposed to be?"

"It's curtains," he said, the "duh" unspoken yet understood.

"You want to go as window treatments?"

"No. That makes no sense. We can go as opening night. We can each wear one panel. We can pull them apart and reveal the moon and stars on T-shirts. Get it? *Opening night?*" He looked so proud of himself she almost hated to burst his bubble.

"I do. But it's way too complicated. If you have to explain the costume then it's no good."

"That's what you said before. I still disagree about the Milk Duds."

"Me dressing as a carton of milk and you as an unexploded grenade? Do people even eat Milk Duds anymore?"

"I can't believe you just asked that. They're one of my favorite candies ever."

"Sorry for offending the junk food addict in you."

"You're forgiven." Caleb looked at the curtains again. "I still think opening night can work."

She shook her head. "It would be too hard to dance. And how would we go to the bathroom if we were stuck together? And before you ask, I still don't want to go as radio waves. I'm not wearing a box with painted-on knobs while you get to wear big hands. Nor do I want to switch."

"I have the perfect solution. I can smoke a cigar and wear glasses. You can wear a slip. You can dance in that and going to the bathroom won't be an issue." He brushed his hands together as if it was a done deal.

She frowned. "I don't get it."

"I'll be Freud. We'll be—"

"—a Freudian slip."

"Yes." He smiled.

"No."

"Well, then, I'm fresh out of ideas."

"Thank goodness."

"I'm ignoring you," he said with a laugh and began searching through the shelves. Clearly he was not offended by her comment. But then, they had been kidding each other all morning. He'd arrived at her house bright and early this morning. She'd cooked waffles, eggs and sausage. After taking his first bite, Caleb had begun proposing one wacky idea after the other, taking up from where he'd left off yesterday. Many of the ideas had been clever, but she didn't see how they could actually make the costumes. Given that the party was tonight, they were running out of time.

"How about we go to the party *as* a party?" Caleb asked.

She'd been digging through a box. She stopped and looked at him. "What does that even mean?"

"You can use that fabric to make a dartboard shirt. You can wear pants and still be able to dance. People play darts at parties."

"What kind of parties do you go to?"

"Okay. Not a party. A sports bar."

"That's good. That has possibility. What will you go as?"

He held up a T-shirt with a vintage beer logo on front. "I can go as a bottle of beer."

"A T-shirt is not really much of a costume."

"Or…" He held up the curtains in his other hand as if weighing their options. "Opening night?"

"When you put it like that…"

Caleb laughed.

"I actually like the idea of a beer bottle T-shirt, but I think we can do a bit better than that. I can make a hat that looks like a bottle cap." She rubbed her hands together. "This is going to be so good."

They paid for everything and then headed back to her house. She pulled her sewing machine out of the closet, then searched through her fabric box until she found what she needed. Fortunately the costumes were pretty simple and it only took an hour or so to complete. Caleb insisted on making them something to eat while she sewed. It felt nice to have a man prepare a meal for her. Having him bustling about her kitchen should have felt strange, but it didn't. It felt cozy.

She was pressing the last seam when he set a plate on the edge of the ironing board. "Dinner is served."

"Just in time. I'm finished. And starved." She washed her hands and then picked up her plate. They sat on the couch and started on their grilled cheese sandwiches, salad and tomato soup.

"This meal is my specialty," he said.

"And one of my favorites. I generally don't mind

cooking, but there are times when I'm too hungry to make a big dinner."

"I get it. My mother loves to cook and she's taught me how to make a number of different dishes. But unlike her, I don't like spending hours in the kitchen unless I'm baking a pie. Fifteen minutes is all I'm willing to do."

"Same."

"My mom makes a big Sunday dinner every week. I wouldn't want to hurt her feelings by not taking home leftovers. Those generally last a day or so."

Faith smirked. "You're such a good son."

"I try to be."

He sounded so serious that Faith looked up, spoon in hand. "You are," she repeated. "I suspect you're feeling guilty again about looking for your bio dad. Let me remind you to stop it now."

He was silent for a moment, staring into space. Then he smiled. "Thanks. I needed that."

"Of course."

He smiled and polished off the last of his sandwich. "That should hold me until the party. Hopefully, they'll have more than candy."

Faith laughed. "They will. Remember, we can't leave until after they announce the winners."

"If we don't win, don't blame me. I still think we should have gone as movie tickets."

"Or bowling pins. I know." She waved him off with a stifled smile. "Don't worry. I won't get upset if we don't win. It's all in good fun. Plus, this will be a way for you to meet some of the people in town."

"True."

They grabbed their dishes and put them in the kitchen sink. "Let's get changed. We don't want to be late."

Faith showed Caleb to her guest room where he could change then she put on her costume in her bedroom. She stood in front of her full-length mirror and checked her appearance. Not too shabby for a last-minute job.

She grabbed her purse, then headed for the living room. Caleb was already there, sitting on her sofa. He stood and applauded when Faith entered. "You look so good. I have no doubt you'll win first place."

Faith took a bow. She'd made the dartboard out of two foldable paper fans, covering them with black and red cloth. Now she closed the fans and unfastened them from her shirt and then dropped them into her large purse where they wouldn't get bent.

"You look pretty good yourself." She adjusted the silver cap on his head. "I'm not much of a beer drinker, but if I was, yours is definitely the brand I would pick up."

"You say the sweetest things." Caleb grinned and held out his arm. "Shall we get this show on the road?"

Faith looped her arm with his. "Absolutely."

Once they were settled in his truck, Faith leaned back against the seat and smiled at him. "We're going to have the best time."

"I'm already having the best time," Caleb said. "Being with you is always fun."

Those quietly spoken words made Faith's heart skip a beat. Caleb wasn't flirting or spouting a line. She heard the sincerity in his tone and felt it. His openness gave her the courage to be as honest as he'd been. "I feel the same way about you."

Caleb looked pleased as he turned his attention back

to the road. Neither of them spoke for a while as if basking in the glow of their shared feelings and trying to figure out what came next. At least that was what she was doing.

When they arrived at the Bronco Community Center, Caleb parked and Faith reassembled her dartboard costume before they entered the building. Strips of black and orange crepe paper dangled from the ceiling. The walls were decorated with black cats, orange jack-o'-lanterns and colorful scarecrows. Bales of hay were stacked at random intervals down the hall. The lighting was dim, casting spooky shadows on the walls.

"They went all out," Caleb said.

"Of course. We don't do things halfway here in Bronco."

"It's nice that the town has the funds to decorate this way. It's a little thing, but it goes a long way when you set the mood. The right ambience makes a difference." He frowned. "I wish we could afford special events like this in Tenacity. I think it would help strengthen the sense of community and build morale. Maybe more young people would be inclined to stay. But when you only have so much money, choices have to be made. Do you spend the cash on a three-hour party or do you fill potholes?"

"I get your point. Hopefully, Tenacity will find the magic it needs to increase the funds in its coffers. That way they won't have to choose. They can do both things."

He nodded. "Enough talk about that. We're at a party, so let's enjoy ourselves."

They followed the sound of up-tempo music down the hall and then stepped into the party room. The decorations were just as elaborate as the ones in the hallways.

Round tables interspersed with orange and black tablecloths were arranged around the perimeter of the room with a dance floor in the middle.

The dance floor was filled with costumed merrymakers moving to the song blaring over the speakers. There were only adults present. There was a separate party for the kids in another room.

"Do you want to find a seat or would you rather dance?" Caleb asked.

"Dance. Definitely dance." Faith shimmied her shoulders and wiggled her hips. It had been a long time since she'd been to a party much less danced and she didn't want to wait another minute.

"Well, then, let's go. I don't want to keep you from shaking your groove thing."

Faith laughed. "My *groove* thing?"

"You know what I mean." He wiggled his eyebrows suggestively as his gaze swept over her hips. Butterflies immediately began soaring around her stomach and the blood began to pulse in her veins. Caleb held out his hand and led her to the dance floor where they managed to find a spot that wasn't too crowded. They immediately began to move to the beat and Faith was pleased to note that Caleb could more than hold his own. One song blended into another and they danced to several up-tempo tunes until the notes of a slow song filled the air.

Caleb extended his arms and Faith held up a hand. She unpinned her dartboard costume before going into his arms, sinking into him. She leaned her head against his chest and sighed as his arms wrapped around her. She felt his heart beat beneath her ear. It was steady and strong. His torso was hard and muscular and she felt his abs move in and out as he breathed. His cologne hinted of the outdoors. It smelled so good she would be happy to stand here breathing it in all night. Everything about this moment was perfect and she wished it could last forever.

After the last notes of the song faded away, the DJ announced that finger food was now being served. Faith and Caleb joined the buffet lines at the front of the room. Faith introduced Caleb to the people around them and they chatted until they reached the trays of food. Faith and Caleb grabbed glasses of fruit punch and filled their clear plastic plates with mini subs, pizza rolls, chips and carrots.

They were headed for a dining table when Faith spotted Elizabeth sitting with her rancher husband, Jake McCreery. Faith turned to Caleb. "Hey, there's my sister. Do you mind sitting with her and her husband?"

"That's fine with me."

They crossed the room and stood beside two empty chairs. "Can we join you?"

Elizabeth smiled, stood, and then embraced her sister. "You know you can. I didn't expect to see you here. You said you weren't coming."

"It was a last-minute decision." Faith introduced Jake to Caleb and then they sat down.

Faith popped a sausage pizza roll into her mouth. *Delicious.* "Are the kids here?"

"Of course. The five of them are in the kids' party. Although Halloween is becoming more popular in Australia, the girls and I never made a big deal of it. They were over the moon when Jake's kids told them how they celebrate here."

"I imagine they're thrilled to be filling up on pizza and candy," Faith said.

"You know it. Dressing up as mermaids with Molly was the icing on the cake."

"I bet they look so cute."

"They do."

Faith glanced from Elizabeth to Jake. "And where are your costumes?"

"I love a good party as much as the next person," Elizabeth said, "but wearing a costume is where I draw the line."

"That explains why you came as a rodeo star."

"It was either that or a tired mother."

Faith shook her head and then turned to her brother-in-law. "And what are you supposed to be, Jake?"

Jake shrugged. "I'm a rancher. Can't you tell?"

"I tried to convince Faith to come as a rodeo star," Caleb said, "but she shot me down."

"My sister always has to do things the hard way," Elizabeth said.

"Trust me, I know," Caleb said and then began telling them about the costumes that Faith had vetoed.

Jake laughed. "My boys would have definitely preferred to go costume shopping with you instead of me. They had to settle for coming as superheroes. Next year I'll get with you for ideas."

"As long as you and Caleb are the ones making the costumes," Faith said as Elizabeth nodded in agreement. "Those brilliant suggestions of his will be hard to make."

Caleb held up his hands in front of him. "Sorry. I'm just the idea guy. Manufacturing is a separate department."

The others laughed. As they talked, they enjoyed the tasty finger food and drinks. Several of their friends came up and spoke to them and Faith was pleased to note how well Caleb fit in with everyone.

"He's definitely a keeper," Rylee Parker, one of Faith's friends, said as they sat together. Faith hadn't seen her friend since the Golden Buckle Rodeo and they took a moment to catch up.

Faith laughed and glanced over at Caleb. He was talking with Jake so Faith didn't have to worry about him overhearing. "We're having fun now. I'm not making plans for the future."

"You might want to rethink that. Good men don't come along every day." Rylee glanced at her engagement ring, a smile lighting her face. She looked over at her fiancé, Shep Dalton, who was talking with one of his brothers before looking back at Faith.

"Speaking of good men, how are the wedding plans coming along?" Faith asked.

"Good. But busy. With searching for a dress, choosing the menu for the reception, and so much more, I barely have a free minute. Not to mention work. I'm busy working on the Mistletoe Rodeo." Rylee was the marketing director for the Bronco Convention Center where the rodeo was held.

"I'd volunteer to help but I don't know the first thing about weddings."

Rylee glanced at Caleb and then back at Faith. "I have a feeling that might change soon."

"You're as bad as the Hawkins women."

"I'll take that as a compliment," Rylee said, before she gave Faith a hug and walked away to join her fiancé.

Faith was still contemplating Rylee's comment about Caleb when the DJ announced the judges were about to award the prizes. Faith looked toward the makeshift stage where the judges, holding clipboards, were huddled. The room began to buzz as everyone speculated who would win. The head judge approached the microphone and a hush came over the room. Faith and Caleb exchanged grins and he lifted his hands to show his crossed fingers.

Before the judge could make an announcement, a person dressed in a purple floor-length costume and face mask entered the room. Gray hair flowed around her shoulders and big earrings dangled from her ears. There was something vaguely familiar about the way the woman moved, but Faith couldn't put her finger on what it was. The masked woman slowly strode around the room as if searching for someone. Then, without saying a word, she turned and walked out the door.

All of a sudden the room was abuzz and people spoke over each other.

"Did you see her?" a man called.

"Was it her?" a woman asked in an excited voice. "Was it Winona?"

"I couldn't tell with the mask. But it could have been."

"Somebody needs to catch up with her and find out."

"Where is Stanley? Somebody should call him and let him know that Winona was here."

"What's going on?" Caleb asked.

"People think that woman was Winona Cobbs," Jake said. When it was clear the name didn't mean anything to Caleb he continued. "Winona went missing several months ago, hours before her wedding to Stanley Sanchez."

"So she's a runaway bride?" Caleb asked.

"Nothing like that," Elizabeth corrected him. "I was at her bridal shower. Winona was as excited as any bride I've ever seen. In fact, she expressed regret for making her fiancé wait so long to finally set a date. She loves Stanley. There's no way she would simply disappear without a word to him."

"So, what do people think happened?"

"Speculation is running rampant but nobody really has a clue. You know how people love to be the first to know something and then spread their information around even if there are no facts to support it. Winona's been gone since July and with each passing day, the stories grow a little bit more desperate and more outrageous."

"Winona is a little bit eccentric, but she's well liked in town," Jake added.

"Well, if she's back in Bronco, maybe she'll explain where she's been," Faith said.

"I hope so," Elizabeth said.

The commotion gradually died down and a man Faith didn't recognize returned to the room. His breathing was heavy and it took a minute for him to catch his breath. The room grew quiet again as everyone waited to hear what he had to say. "I don't know if that was Winona or not. By the time I got into the hall, she was out of sight. I searched the whole building. Then I checked the parking lot. I even walked around the block but she was gone."

"So you didn't get a look up close?" The woman's

voice was unfamiliar, but Faith recognized the sorrow and disappointment in it.

"No," the man admitted.

"But if that was her, I'm sure she'll let us know in her own time," someone else said.

"And if it wasn't?"

"Then we're in the same place we were an hour ago, wondering what happened to Winona."

That comment was not especially satisfying, but it was the truth.

After the potential sighting, the judge announced the winners of the contest, which Faith had to admit now seemed anticlimactic. She and Caleb didn't win anything, but they were having too much fun to care. The music resumed and after a bit of a lull, the gloomy mood lifted and once more people returned to the dance floor.

"I hate to be a party pooper, but I think it's time for us to grab the kids and head home," Elizabeth said as she got their attention.

"Already?" Faith asked. She'd been having a good time with her sister and her brother-in-law.

"I'm afraid so. Remember, our kids are little. It's already past the twins' and Ben's bedtime." Elizabeth's daughters were five and Jake's son Ben was six. His other two kids were eight and ten. Not exactly the age to party the night away.

"I hope you aren't expecting them to go right to sleep."

Elizabeth grimaced. "With all the sugar they've eaten tonight? No. I dream big, but not that big."

"We can always let them run around the backyard. That ought to help them burn off some energy," Jake suggested with a mischievous grin.

"Or we can drive around with the heat on high," Elizabeth countered. "That might make them drowsy."

Faith and Caleb exchanged glances as they laughed at the other couple. "Tell them all good-night for me," Faith said.

"I will. Of course, you can always come into the kids' party room and do it yourself."

Faith shook her head. "I'll pass. I can only imagine how hectic and loud it is in there."

Elizabeth laughed. "Chicken."

Faith flapped her arms like wings and squawked.

Elizabeth hugged Faith and whispered, "I'll catch up with you later. I need an update on this romance of yours."

"It's not a romance," Faith whispered back, sounding more definite than she felt.

Elizabeth only nodded as she stepped away.

"It was good meeting you," Jake said to Caleb.

"Same."

Caleb and Faith watched as the couple left, arms around each other. Then Faith and Caleb headed for the dance floor, and joined a line dance. When the song ended, several people began streaming out the door. Most of them were parents who no doubt were picking up their children from the kids' party. Since neither she nor Caleb had children, they were free to party for the rest of the night. Even so, all too soon, the last song ended. Faith and Caleb put on their coats and joined the exodus to the parking lot.

"I had such a good time tonight," Faith said once they were ensconced in Caleb's truck.

"So did I," Caleb said.

As they rode back to Faith's house, they recounted the highlights, laughing as they talked about the other costumes they'd seen. A good number had been clever, and quite a few had been elaborate. Faith had to admit that the winners of the contests had deserved their victories.

"We'll win next year," Caleb said, "but we'll have to get an earlier start."

Faith tried not to read too much into that comment, but she couldn't stop her heart from skipping a beat. Nor could she stop the hope that bloomed inside her. Was Caleb planning on being in her life a year from now? Did she want him to be?

Caleb parked in front of Faith's house and her body began to tingle. It was getting harder and harder to keep her feelings for Caleb friendly. The attraction was simply too strong. While she wasn't interested in a romance, perhaps they could have a casual relationship. After all, they were both adults. There was no reason they couldn't have a physical relationship while keeping their hearts out of it. That is, if Caleb was amenable.

Caleb had already made it clear that he didn't have the bandwidth for anything serious. With everything going on in his life, she believed him. Weren't men supposed to be expert at keeping the physical and emotional separate? Maybe Caleb would be able to do that.

Caleb parked in front of her house, then glanced over at her. His eyes were dark and mysterious. "I suppose I need to say good-night," he said. Faith heard the reluctance in his voice.

"You don't have to. You can always come inside for a while."

Caleb grinned. "I was hoping you would say that."

They climbed out of the truck and walked side by side up the stairs and into the house. After hanging their jackets in the closet, Faith gestured for Caleb to have a seat. She rubbed her hands over the front of her thighs. "Would you like a drink?"

"I wouldn't mind."

"Good. I'm in the mood for some warm cider."

He frowned. "That's not my idea of a good drink, but don't let that stop you."

"The thought never crossed my mind." She smiled. "What can I get for you?"

"I wouldn't say no to coffee."

"Of course."

She quickly made their beverages and returned to the living room. They sat side by side on the sofa, his denim-clad leg brushing against hers. Her skin heated at the contact and the blood began to race through her veins. She'd been attracted to men before, but it hadn't felt anything like this. In the past, she'd never had a problem controlling her body and thoughts. Caleb's simplest touch made her burn with desire and sent her imagination running wild. Faith had to face facts. Caleb Strom was irresistible. And she was tired of trying to keep him at a distance.

Faith glanced out the corner of her eye and caught Caleb staring at her. She turned her head in his direction, expecting him to look away. He didn't. Instead he met her stare head-on. The heat in his dark eyes melted her bones to liquid and her hand shook, sending cider sloshing over the side of her mug.

Caleb took her mug, set it on the coffee table, then placed his next to hers. With each passing second, the longing she'd fought to contain grew stronger, threatening to overwhelm her, and her breathing became shallow. He sat back and she looked into Caleb's face, noting the intense desire on his face. Then, as one, they reached out for each other. Their lips met in a hot, passionate kiss that turned the fire inside her into a raging inferno. She pulled him closer, needing to feel more of him, but no matter how close she pressed against his body, she couldn't get enough of him.

Her heart was pounding and blood was racing through her veins. Unexpectedly Caleb broke the kiss. A cry of protest burst from her lips. Confused and vibrating with desire, she reached out to pull his face back to hers. He took her hands and held them in his. He looked into her eyes, his own hazy with yearning. "We need to slow down before I can't stop."

"And if I don't want to stop?"

His chest rose as he inhaled deeply. Her eyes were drawn to the muscles his shirt barely contained. She'd run her hands over his chest and knew just how strong and firm it was. "You need to be sure, Faith. Because as much as I want you, as much as I like you, I can't offer you a relationship. You deserve commitment. Actually, you deserve the world."

"I'm well aware of your limitations, Caleb. I have similar ones of my own. I'm not willing to put my heart on the line right now. But I am willing to have a casual relationship. No strings. No expectations. No risk of heartache. But a whole lot of fun. That is, if you are willing."

He pressed a searing kiss against her lips, sending a

flow of heat throughout her body. "I'm not just willing. I'm completely able."

She stood and held out her hand. He took it without hesitation and they raced up the stairs to her bedroom.

Caleb blinked at the sunlight streaming though the curtains. For a moment he didn't know where he was. The warm woman lying beside him instantly cleared that up. He was in Faith's bed. He closed his eyes as pleasant memories of the night they'd just shared flashed through his mind. He'd slept with women in the past, although not nearly as many as people tended to believe—but he'd never found making love as fulfilling as he had with Faith.

Faith was a generous and spontaneous lover. What could have been an awkward first time had been fun. Their friendly and comfortable relationship had not stopped at her bedroom door. They'd been completely in tune with each other. After satisfying their physical needs, they'd talked and laughed late into the night until Faith had fallen asleep with her head on his chest. Now, despite how at ease they'd been with each other last night, he experienced a bit of trepidation. It was easy for Faith to say she could keep things casual *before* making love. Would she actually be able to do that now that she'd given herself to him so fully?

"Stop thinking so hard," Faith said, startling him.

"I didn't know you were awake."

She stretched languidly and opened her eyes. "I wasn't. But you tensed up and I could practically hear the wheels whirling in your head."

He glanced at her face. Even without a hint of makeup, she was positively gorgeous. "Is that right?"

She propped herself on one elbow and looked down at him. She walked two fingers across his chest, leaving a trail of fire behind. "Yes."

He captured her fingers and brushed a kiss against her palm. "So, what am I thinking about?"

"You're worried that I won't be able to keep from falling in love with irresistible you. You're afraid that I can't separate the emotional from the physical. But I can. I want things to be casual between us. More than that, I *need* for things to be casual. That's the only way that this works for me."

Relief washed over him at her words even as his ego chafed a bit. A small part of him wished that she would fall madly in love with him. That same part knew he could fall head over heels in love with her in a heartbeat. But then what? He wasn't in a position to give her the love and attention that she deserved. And he certainly couldn't put her on hold.

"Then we're in agreement," he said finally.

"Yes." She sat up, pulling the striped sheet up over her perfect breasts, hiding them from view. "I suppose we should get up."

He sat up and dropped a kiss on her bare shoulder, then nuzzled her neck. "How about I take you out to breakfast?"

"I wish I could take you up on that. I'm meeting my sisters to practice for an upcoming rodeo in an hour." She gave him a glance that set his blood on fire. "But there's time to shower before I need to hit the road. You're invited. Unless you'd rather grab your clothes and go."

Caleb looked around. His clothes were scattered around the bedroom, evidence of the rush they'd been in last night. His T-shirt was draped over the arm of a chair, coming close to dragging the floor. His pants were inside out near the closet and tangled with Faith's.

Not waiting for an answer, Faith tossed off the sheet, then got out of the bed wearing nothing but a smile. She glanced over her shoulder at him, an invitation in her eyes, one brow raised in a dare. Caleb was never one to walk away from a challenge, especially one that came wrapped in such a delectable package.

Standing, and as naked as she was, he walked across the room, his eyes never breaking contact with hers. He held out his arm and they walked side by side to her cozy bathroom. The tiled shower was small, but big enough for two and Caleb stepped aside as Faith turned on the water and tested it with her hand. When she found the temperature satisfactory, she stepped inside and winked at Caleb, who followed her.

She grabbed a bar of soap and a washcloth and he did the same. Once their cloths were lathered up, they began to wash each other. He'd touched her in every place possible last night, his hands often pausing in the most sensitive spots. Watching her dissolve with desire had been extremely pleasurable. Even so, rubbing the terry-cloth square against her smooth brown skin was just as exciting and stimulating today.

Faith rubbed her cloth across his torso, her sensual touch leaving a trail of suds behind. She followed the cloth with a fingernail, dragging it through the bubbles. The water from the showerhead pounded on his back and shoulders, running in rivulets down his legs and to the drain. The heat rose between them as they washed each other. Her hand wandered down his chest and over his stomach, and his muscles clenched in response. Flames of longing licked inside him and the pounding water was powerless to douse it.

What started out as harmful play quickly turned passionate and their laughter faded away. Caleb captured Faith's lips in a searing kiss. When she sighed and opened her mouth to him, his desire raged even hotter. He lifted her into his arms and she wrapped her legs around his waist. Stopping to turn off the water, he carried her from the bathroom and into the bedroom. He tossed her onto the bed, then jumped in beside her. Familiar with her body, he knew exactly what to do to drive her wild and focused on giving her the utmost pleasure.

"I could get used to starting the day like this," Faith said some time later.

"You and me both."

Her stomach growled loudly and she frowned. "Of course, that might mean I'd miss more meals than I can afford to."

"Nah. It just means we need to wake up earlier." He brushed a kiss on her damp shoulder and then sat up. "But that's a sacrifice I'm willing to make."

She ran a hand across his abs, a devilish expression on her face. He forced himself to resist. Covering her hand with his, he stopped her progress. "Not now. We need to get dressed so we get out of here. You have to meet your sisters, remember."

"I do." She scrambled from the bed and headed for her bathroom. After watching her walk away with a bit of extra swing to her hips, Caleb gathered his clothes and headed for the guest bathroom. The shower stall was smaller but it served its purpose. He quickly washed and dressed, then went downstairs to wait for Faith.

There were lots of knickknacks and pictures on the tables and bookshelves. He picked up a framed photo of Faith. Dressed in rodeo gear, she looked to be about twelve or thirteen. She held the reins of her horse in one hand and a giant trophy in the other. Her smile was wide and her eyes shone with pride at her victory.

He set down the picture and picked up another. She was older in this picture—but only slightly taller. The outfit was different, but the expression on her face was the same. Instead of a trophy, she was holding a belt buckle. Time had changed a few things, but she was still a champion.

Faith stepped into the room. He turned to look at her and smiled. She was dressed in a floral flannel shirt that she'd tucked into faded jeans that showcased her small waist. Even dressed casually, she was temptation personified. But more than lust, he felt a strong—and growing—affection for her.

He had agreed to keep things casual between them. Now he wondered just how long he would be able to keep it up.

Chapter Eleven

Faith waited on the porch for her mother to answer the door. As she did, her mind replayed the message Suzie had left for her earlier that day. "I need you to stop by after practice. We need to talk in person."

Although she'd told herself not to worry, she couldn't stop the thoughts that assaulted her. Was Suzie sick? That idea, though terrifying, didn't make sense. Why would she only want to talk to Faith and not all of her daughters? Or at least the four of them that lived in Bronco? It had to be something else. While she was trying to come up with an alternative answer, the door swung open.

"Sorry. I didn't realize that the door was locked. Come on in." Suzie stepped aside and Faith quickly entered.

"Thanks." Faith looked at her mother. As usual, Suzie looked radiant. Her ash-blond hair brushed against her shoulders. Her fair skin was just as clear and glowed as always. Suzie was the picture of health. Even so, Faith's nerves were still on edge. She couldn't bear not knowing for another moment. "What's going on? Is everything okay? You aren't sick, are you?"

Suzie gave a little laugh. "No. Whatever gave you an idea like that?"

Relief surged through Faith's body and she sighed before answering. "Your message was a bit cryptic to say the least. 'We need to talk. In person.'"

Suzie shook her head as she and Faith sat on the sofa. "I forgot how dramatic you can be. You always did have a wild imagination."

"And that imagination got the best of me," Faith admitted. "So if there's nothing wrong, what did you need to talk to me about so urgently? What couldn't we discuss over the phone?"

A sober expression replaced the smile on her mother's face and Faith's stomach began to churn again.

"I was thinking about your friend, Caleb."

Faith's heart skipped a beat at the mere mention of Caleb's name. Images of the two of them wrapped in each other's arms flashed through her mind. His touch had been erotic and his kisses had been stimulating. Making love with Caleb had been more pleasurable than anything she'd ever experienced before. She was longing to feel that way again. Before she could get flustered, she forced her mind back to the conversation at hand. "What about Caleb?"

"I heard that the two of you were together at the Halloween party."

"Word travels fast."

"I take it that you like him a lot."

"I do. You don't have a problem with that, do you?" Faith frowned. Was this why her mother needed to talk in person?

Suzie shook her head. "Not at all."

"Then what is it?"

"I was thinking about his search for his biological father."

Of course Suzie would wonder how things were going. She had a big heart. "It's not going that well. He's hit a wall. But he's not going to give up. He's determined to find his biological dad."

"That's not a good idea."

"What do you mean? Why do you say that?"

"He should stop searching."

"Stop? Why?" That was the last thing Faith expected her mother to say.

Suzie was quiet for a long moment. She picked at the cuticle of her perfectly manicured nail, then brushed imaginary lint from her pants. Finally she looked up at Faith. She appeared to have a hard time meeting Faith's eyes. "I wasn't entirely honest with you before. I know who Caleb's biological father is."

"You do? How did you find out? Who is he? Is he alive?" Faith asked excitedly. She couldn't wait to tell Caleb. He was going to be so happy.

"Yes, he's alive. And I'm not going to tell you who he is."

"Why not?"

"Because I have no doubt that you'll go straight from here to Caleb. You'll tell him. I don't want you to. It will only cause him pain."

"How do you know that?"

"Because I knew the man." Suzie's voice was flat.

"You knew him?" Faith asked, at once outraged and disappointed in her mother. "You said you hadn't heard a word about an adoption. You told me that you were so busy raising your family that you didn't have time to keep up with gossip."

Suzie's cheeks pinkened. "I remember what I said, so you don't need to replay it for me. And I'm not telling you his name. That's not why I wanted to talk."

"Then why?" Faith folded her arms over her chest.

"To get you to convince Caleb to stop looking."

Faith shook her head. "I won't do that."

"And I won't tell you his name."

"Forget about his name for the moment. What *are* you willing to tell me about him?"

"He wasn't a good man."

"I'm willing to accept that you believe that. But I need more than that."

Suzie shook her head and pressed her lips together.

"Please, Mom. What aren't you telling me?"

Suzie sighed. "I knew Caleb's biological mother."

Faith's heart stuttered. "Really?"

"Yes. She was such a sweet woman. A girl really. She was in her teens when I met her. And she was only twenty when Caleb was born. She loved Caleb's father with her whole heart. There was nothing she wouldn't do for that man." Suzie's voice turned bitter. Hard. "But he didn't want to make their relationship public. Even after she had the baby, he insisted on keeping their marriage a secret. Now, she adored him, so naturally she did as he asked. All she wanted was to be with him. If he was happy, then so was she."

"So their marriage remained a secret," Faith surmised.

"Yes."

"Then how did you know about it?"

"I told you. I was friends with Caleb's birth mother, so I saw everything firsthand." She paused only a moment before she continued. "After she died, Caleb's father left the child behind. He continued to travel on the rodeo circuit and never looked back. I doubt he ever thought about that baby again."

Faith thought of Caleb's need to find his father and decided to try again. "You should tell me his father's name."

Suzie shook her head. "No good will come from Caleb getting in touch with the man."

"I could understand keeping the information a secret if Caleb was still a child and needed protection. But he's a grown man. It should be his decision."

"He's my friend's son. She's not here, so she can't protect him. But I can. I'm not going to do something that I know will hurt him. I owe her that much."

"You said she loved Caleb's father. She wouldn't want you to keep them apart."

Suzie folded her arms against her chest, a move that Faith recognized. She was not going to budge from her stubborn position. "Did you hear a word I said? Surely you don't think this is the kind of person Caleb needs in his life."

"Mom," Faith said, gently, reaching out to touch her mother's arm. "Try to put yourself in Caleb's position. He only wants to know more about his birth family. He needs to know where he came from. Surely as someone who was adopted, you know how important that is."

"Are you saying that you don't know where you came from? Or where you belong? That you don't feel like you're a part of the Hawkins family?" Suzie sounded at once angry and hurt. That wasn't at all what Faith wanted. She'd simply been trying to get Suzie to put herself in Caleb's shoes.

"No, Mom. And I believe you know that. But you were adopted as a teenager, so you know about your birth parents."

"Yes. And they were no picnic. Getting adopted by Hattie Hawkins was the best thing that ever happened to me. I can't tell you how glad I am that the state of Oklahoma didn't see fit to get in the way of that."

Faith nodded. Hattie was Black and allowing her to adopt a white teenager had been unusual for the times. Perhaps her fame on the rodeo circuit was part of the reason. That, and the fact that Suzie had been dirt-poor and without other family.

"They might not have been the best people in the world, but you knew them. You don't have to wonder who you look like. You don't have to wonder what behaviors you inherited from them."

"None. Thank God. If I act like anyone, it's my mother, Hattie Hawkins."

Faith blew out a breath. Suzie didn't like to talk about her birth parents at all. As far as she was concerned, they weren't worth remembering. Her anger toward them and her bad childhood were no doubt coloring her perspective now. She truly believed that she was protecting Caleb from unnecessary pain. Suzie didn't understand that having unanswered questions was painful too.

"In his position, I would wonder about my birth parents," Faith said.

"Meaning what?"

"Just what I said. I would wonder what they looked

like. I'd wonder about their likes and dislikes. I'd question if they would want to know me, or if they never gave me a second thought once I had been adopted. So many things would eat at me. Maybe not all the time, but often enough. It wouldn't keep me from loving you and Dad, or being happy with my life, but it would be there. Like a ghost haunting me."

"You know your birth parents. Or at least your birth mother."

"Yes. And because I know her, I understand why she gave me up for adoption. In her position, I might have done the same thing. Her life could have turned out so differently if she would have had to care for a child at her age. Instead, she gave me to a loving family."

Suzie huffed out a breath. "And your point is?"

Faith covered her mother's hands with her own, giving them a gentle squeeze before replying. When she did, her voice was soft. "My point is that Caleb needs to find out about his past. You should help him."

Suzie pulled her hands away. "No. I can't do that."

"Is that your final word?"

"Yes."

"In that case, I'll see you later."

Feeling helpless, Faith kissed her mother's cheek and left. She didn't know what else she could do or what else she could say. And who knew—perhaps Suzie was right. After all, she'd been there and seen it all. Caleb did say his father had wanted to keep his identity a secret from him. Perhaps it was best if Caleb didn't meet the man.

That thought stayed with Faith the rest of the day and long into the night. She wished she knew what to do. One thing was certain. She didn't want to cause Caleb unnecessary pain. She considered telling him what her mother had said about his father, but decided against it. Besides, what did Faith actually know? She didn't know the identity of Caleb's father; she didn't know his mother's name. Most importantly, she didn't know how to convince her mother to share the information she was holding close to her heart.

When you added it all up, Faith didn't know anything. At least nothing helpful.

Caleb smiled as he exited the highway and turned onto the ramp leading to Bronco. Although his father had told him he could take a leave of absence while he tried to make contact with Brooks Langtree, Caleb had decided against it. Who knew how long that would take. From what Caleb could tell, Langtree had left Bronco sometime after the Golden Buckle Rodeo ended. Not that it made a difference. Caleb hadn't been able to reach Brooks when he had been in town.

Even though he was disappointed about his failure to connect with Brooks, Caleb was very happy with how things were going with Faith. Dating her was the most fun he'd had in his life. No other woman had made him laugh the way Faith did. Not that every conversation was a party. They'd also discussed serious matters. He'd been impressed by her insight and compassion. He appreciated the way she made him consider different perspectives.

The past week without her had dragged, but going to work had been the right thing to do. Running the store took a lot of effort and was more than Nathan could handle alone. Not only that, Caleb enjoyed the work. Strom and Son Farm and Feed Supply was a successful business and Caleb intended to keep it that way. His family, employees and the citizens of Tenacity were depending on him and he wasn't going to let them down.

But it was Friday night and the store was closed and the weekend belonged to him. Faith had invited him to stay at her house, but he'd turned her down, choosing to stay at the B and B again. Staying with Faith would have flown in the face of their decision to keep things casual. Caleb didn't want to send mixed signals. Crossing lines could lead to confusion and pain, something they were each trying to avoid.

Caleb checked into his room and then phoned Faith. His pulse sped up as he waited for her to answer. *That was ridiculous.* This wasn't some great love story. They were just two friends getting together tonight. Their plans were nothing special. They were going to go to Doug's, a local dive bar that Faith liked and wanted to show him, for burgers. It wasn't romantic, but then, he wasn't aiming for romance.

Faith answered on the second ring. The moment Caleb heard her voice, a sense of contentment enveloped him and he relaxed. He couldn't quite put his finger on why but just talking to her made his worries fade away.

"Are we still good for tonight?" he asked.

"Of course. I've been looking forward to seeing you all week. I'll be ready in a few minutes."

Just knowing that she was as eager to be together again made the loneliness of being apart worth it.

Faith was standing on her front porch when he arrived. She was dressed in tight jeans, over-the-knee black boots, a cable-knit purple sweater and a purple jacket.

A purple-and-black headband held her hair away from her face. She was even more gorgeous than he remembered and his blood heated. He might not want to become emotionally involved with Faith, but his body had made a deep connection with hers.

He was getting out of his truck when she started jogging down the stairs. When he realized that she wasn't going to stand on formality, he restarted the engine and waited for her to climb in beside him.

"Hi," she said, turning a bright smile on him.

"Hi yourself." Unable to resist, he pressed a gentle kiss against her soft lips. His mouth tingled at the brief contact. The urge to pull her into his arms was strong, but he resisted. The sexual attraction between them was intense. It wouldn't take much to set them both ablaze. They wouldn't make it to their destination if he gave in to temptation now. Besides, there was plenty of time to satisfy that hunger later tonight, so he pulled away from the curb and headed for the bar.

"You're going to love Doug's. It's not fancy, but the food is good. Plus there's a pool table and a small dance floor. Most of the people are regulars, but they're very welcoming of new people."

Though they had either talked or texted every night this past week, they still had a lot of catching up to do. Faith had just finished telling him about an upcoming rodeo she and her sisters were going to compete in when she directed him to park.

"This is Doug's?" he asked, unable to keep the shock from his voice. There wasn't even a sign on the old building. If Faith hadn't pointed it out to him, he would have passed right by.

"Yep. You aren't one to judge a book by its cover, are you?"

"I try not to judge at all."

Faith sighed. "Just when I thought I couldn't like you more than I already do."

Caleb held the door for her and they stepped inside. There were a good number of patrons inside.

Faith and Caleb grabbed a table near the small dance floor where he anticipated they would spend a lot of time tonight. He couldn't decide if he wanted to slow dance and hold her delectable body pressed against his, or if he wanted faster dances where he could watch her wiggle her sexy bottom. Why not both?

"Why not both what?" Faith asked, a confused smile on her face.

"Did I say that out loud?"

Faith nodded. "Yep."

"I was actually thinking of whether I would prefer to dance fast or slow with you."

"Ah. And you decided on both."

"Yes."

She leaned back in her chair and stretched out her curvy legs in front of her, crossing them at the ankles. "You're assuming that I want to dance. I might just want to sit and talk."

"I know you too well to fall for that. You want to dance."

"You're right. I've been looking forward to dancing all week."

The waitress approached their table, took their orders and was back with them before long.

"That's absolutely delicious," Caleb said after swallowing the first bite of his burger.

"Nothing tastes better than that first bite," Faith agreed.

"I didn't say that," Caleb said, staring at Faith's luscious mouth. "I can think of one thing."

Faith's cheeks grew darker as she blushed. Then she gave him a look so hot he felt his temperature rise. "Is that right?"

"You know it. And later I hope to taste it again."

"For dessert?"

"Absolutely."

"I look forward to it."

Anticipation was great and simultaneously terrible. But making love with Faith later would be worth the wait.

After they'd eaten every bit of their burgers and fries, Caleb dumped a handful of quarters in the jukebox and selected a mix of fast and slow songs, and they headed for the tiny dance floor. Watching Faith dance was almost as pleasurable as holding her in his arms and swaying to a ballad. Once the jukebox was quiet, they grabbed pool cues and headed for the pool table.

"I'm a really good player," Faith said, racking the balls.

"Is that right?" Caleb had been putting chalk on his cue. Now he paused, leaned on his stick, and looked at her. "Care to make a friendly wager?"

She looked at him from toes to head. Incredibly, his skin began to warm. It was as if she'd dragged a red hot coal across his body. "What do you have in mind?"

"How about the loser has to do whatever the winner wants?" he suggested.

"For how long? A day? A week?"

He chuckled. “One game. One thing. One time.”

“That’s all? Why? Are you scared you aren’t going to win?”

“Oh, I’m going to win. I just don’t want to take advantage of you. That wouldn’t be gentlemanly.”

She flashed him a grin. “It’s also not gentlemanly to brag, but that doesn’t seem to bother you.”

Unable to resist, he reached out and cupped her chin and caressed her soft cheek. “That wasn’t a brag, sweetheart. That was me giving you a warning. This is your last chance to back out.”

She leaned her face into his hand for a moment. Then she straightened. “Don’t try to distract me.”

“I wouldn’t dream of it.” If anyone was in danger of being distracted, it was him. The way her round bottom filled out her tight jeans was ruining his concentration.

He moved aside as she stepped up to the table. She took her shot, sending two solid balls into the pockets. After she’d taken two more shots, he knew that he was in for a challenge. Good. He liked knowing that winning would require all of his skill.

She took another shot and missed. He lined up his shot and knocked two striped balls into the pockets. And then another. He was clearing the table when she came to stand by him. Her sweet scent wafted over to him, and he glanced over at her, then turned back to the pool table. As he was taking his shot, she dragged her hands over her breasts, smoothing out her sweater, and wiggled her hips. Those moves were so enticing that he momentarily lost track of what he was doing. The stick tapped the cue ball, but the contact wasn’t hard enough to knock his ball into the pocket.

"Oh. Too bad, so sad," Faith said, nudging him aside. "My turn."

He was still sputtering when she took—and made—her next shot. And then sank the eight ball. "I win. It's going to be so good to make you do whatever I want."

"You distracted me on purpose."

She grinned. "All's fair in love and pool."

"I'll remember that."

"Do that."

"What did you have in mind for me to do?"

"I don't know. You'll have to wait and see."

"I can wait. I'm a very patient man."

"Good things come to those who wait." She winked. "Or at least that's what people keep telling me."

They played two more games and he won both of them. "So I guess I get to tell you what to do twice."

She shook her head. "Nope. The bet was for one game. There's one winner. Me."

"In that case, let's leave. Ready to go?"

She nodded and gave him a look hot enough to boil his blood. "I'm more than ready. I'm willing and able."

He took her hand and led her to his truck. His heart thumped hard as he drove to her house where they could be alone. Although he'd had a good time hanging out with her at Doug's, he was looking forward to getting reacquainted with her body.

When he reached her house, he parked and they jumped from the vehicle and dashed across the lawn and up the stairs to her front door. When Faith jammed the key into the lock, he pushed open the door, scooped Faith into his arms and, kicking the door shut, he carried her through the front room and up the stairs to her bedroom. They fell on the bed together, laughing and pulling off each other's clothes.

It took less than a minute for them to shed their clothes and go into each other's arms. As they touched and caressed, the heat inside Caleb grew and intensified until he was near to exploding. Faith cried out in pleasure mere seconds before his cry joined hers. He wrapped her in his arms and pulled her close to him. For now, all was right in his world.

Chapter Twelve

Faith was in trouble. She was falling hard for Caleb. She'd spent the past week trying to convince herself that her feelings hadn't grown, but she knew she was lying to herself. Despite her best intentions, she was unable to keep their relationship purely physical. Somehow her feelings had become involved. She cared about Caleb more than she wanted to. Much more than was safe for her heart. But that was her problem. One that she didn't intend to burden Caleb with. They'd both agreed that there was no room for emotions in this relationship. She couldn't even consider changing the parameters of their relationship when she was keeping a huge secret from him.

She parked and walked to the front door of the B and B. Caleb was waiting for her in the main room. Her heart skipped a beat as she looked at him. No matter how much time she spent with him, she was always struck by how handsome he was.

They met in the middle of the room and he brushed a gentle kiss against her lips. As usual, desire surged through her and a tingling sensation danced up and down her spine.

He led her to the room he was renting and she looked around. The room was quite charming.

"How are you today?" he asked, closing the door behind him.

"Good now that we're together." Faith draped her arms over his shoulders. Looping them around his neck, she pulled his head down for a proper kiss. He didn't disappoint.

Slowly, they ended the kiss and she looked in his eyes. "What's the plan for the day?"

It was Sunday afternoon and he would be returning to Tenacity in the morning. She wished he could stay longer, but she knew he needed to go to work. So did she. She wanted to be at her best in her upcoming rodeo.

"I thought we could go to the corn maze and then visit the Happy Hearts Animal Rescue."

Faith smiled. She hadn't visited a corn maze in years. It was always fun getting lost in one and trying to find her way out. Though she wasn't interested in getting a pet, she did enjoy spending time around the animals. "That sounds like fun."

Caleb's room phone rang. Giving her a confused look, he crossed the room and answered it. He listened and then smiled broadly. "Sure. Come on up."

When he ended the call, Caleb stared into space for a few seconds, a smile on his face. Faith tapped him on the shoulder. "Have our plans changed?"

"What?" Caleb blinked. "Sorry. Maybe not changed but definitely delayed. That was actually your grandmother. She's here with something she wants to show me."

Faith wondered how her grandmother knew that

Caleb was staying here. Then she dismissed the question as ridiculous. News traveled fast in Bronco. Plus, there were only so many places in town that Caleb could be staying.

There was a knock on his door. Caleb hurried across the room and then ushered Hattie inside. She was carrying a cloth shopping bag in each hand.

Hattie's eyes darted from Caleb to Faith. She smiled slowly. "I hope I'm not interrupting anything."

"Not at all," Caleb said.

"It's good to see you." Faith kissed her grandmother's cheek. "What do you have there?"

"Patience," Hattie said. "Didn't your parents tell you that good things come to those who wait?"

Faith smiled as she recalled saying those very words to Caleb right before their torrid night of lovemaking. "All the time. But I was the daughter who didn't believe that."

Hattie laughed. "No. Now that I think of it, you weren't very patient. But it's never too late to change that."

"Would you like to sit down?" Caleb asked as he pulled the chair from the desk and turned it to face Hattie.

"I would." Hattie sat down. "Such a gentleman."

Faith sat on the foot of the bed and Caleb sat beside her. He smiled at Hattie. "I have to admit that I'm sharing Faith's curiosity."

"Well, then let me put you both out of your suspense." Hattie leaned one bag against the chair and put the other on her lap. She reached in and pulled out a handful of programs. "After Faith and I talked, I searched through programs of rodeos that I'd participated in."

"You have quite a collection," Caleb said.

"I had quite the career," Hattie said. "I brought programs from rodeos from thirty years ago too. I wasn't competing then but I like keeping a historical record on the evolution of rodeo. I also like keeping souvenirs of rodeos where my daughters and granddaughters competed."

She handed over those to Caleb and then reached inside her tote and pulled out even more. Those she gave to Faith.

"Thank you," Caleb said.

"I figured that looking through these would be a good place to start."

Faith opened the first program and began to flip through the pages. She read through the list of competitors, pausing when she saw her mother's name and picture. Suzie was years younger and had a confident expression on her face. Faith had seen plenty of pictures of her mother in photo albums, but those photos, taken at birthday parties, graduations and Christmas mornings were snapshots of Suzie as a mother. These were of Suzie as a rodeo competitor.

"Are we looking for someone in particular?" Faith asked as she turned the page and continued to peruse the pictures.

"Yes," Hattie said. "But I don't want to influence either of you. I might be seeing something that isn't there. I'll wait to see what you both have to say."

Caleb didn't appear to be listening to the conversation. He was scanning the pages as if looking for a certain individual. He turned a page and stopped. He sucked in a ragged breath and froze.

Hattie walked over and Caleb handed the program to

her. She glanced at the picture and then smiled. "You see what I do."

As if unable to speak, Caleb only nodded.

"What do you see?" Faith asked. Hattie handed her the program. Faith looked at the picture of Brooks Langtree. "Wow. You look exactly like him. In fact, you could be twins."

The expression on Caleb's face said it all. He'd found his birth father. "I've been trying to get in touch with him. His people won't let me near him unless I tell them what I want to talk to him about. Naturally I don't want to do that. This is personal."

"I know Brooks," Hattie said. "I'll have no trouble getting past his gatekeepers. I'll reach out to him for you."

"You'd do that for me?"

"Of course I will," Hattie said. She patted Caleb's hand. "You just leave everything to me."

Caleb's expression was so hopeful that Faith could barely stand to look at him. She hated the idea of that hope being shattered if what her mother had said was true.

"I don't think that's a good idea," Faith blurted out.

Caleb and Hattie looked at her as if she'd suddenly sprouted a second head.

"Why do you say that?" Caleb asked, his voice ringing with the same confusion that was written all over his face.

"What if he doesn't want to meet you? Did you ever think of that? Perhaps he doesn't want to know you at all." Faith tried to control her voice, but as she grew more desperate, her voice reflected that. She glanced at Caleb.

His eyes were wide with surprise. She inhaled and then blew out the breath. She needed to be calm and logical if she intended to convince him.

She grabbed his arm. "He walked away from you when you needed him the most and then forbade the adoption agency to give out any information about him. He hid his relationship with your mother from everyone even after you were born. Your mother adored him and he didn't do right by her then. What makes you think that he will do right by you now?"

Caleb looked at her, no longer surprised by her speech. Now he looked angry. His lips were turned down and his eyes were narrowed. He stepped back, breaking the contact and her hand dropped to her side. "How do you know any of this?"

"Does it matter how I know?"

"Of course it matters." Disappointment and anger mingled in his voice. Then it lowered in warning. "I'll ask you again, Faith. How do you know anything about my past?"

Faith exhaled and then confessed in a weak voice, barely above a whisper. "My mother told me."

His chest rose and fell with his angry inhalations. "When?"

Before she could answer, Hattie interrupted. "I can see that I'm no longer needed in this conversation. I'll leave so the two of you can talk in private."

Caleb nodded. "Thank you so much. I appreciate all of your help. It's nice to know that I can depend on you."

Although he'd been speaking to Hattie, Caleb's last comment was directed at Faith. She felt the sting of his words.

Hattie gave Faith a look that spoke to the depth of her disappointment in her before leaving. Neither Caleb nor Faith spoke until the door was firmly closed.

"Let me explain," Faith implored, reaching out to Caleb. He dodged her hands and took several steps back. The room wasn't very big, but suddenly the gulf between them was a mile wide. She let her hands drop futilely to her side.

"What can you possibly say to defend yourself?"

"I didn't know his identity until just now."

"Right," he said sarcastically. "You know all about my past—more details than even I know—but you didn't know who my father was. Surely you don't expect me to believe that."

"I asked my mother, but she wouldn't identify him."

He looked at her, his eyes so cold she shivered. The warm relationship they had built up might never have happened. "You knew about my father, and my mother, but couldn't be bothered to tell me."

"I didn't know," she continued, needing him to understand the spot she'd been in. "What was I supposed to do?"

"You could have told me."

"Told you what? My mother wouldn't tell me his name. Or anything else about him no matter how many times I asked. And I did ask. The only thing she would say was that he's bad news and it will be best if you keep away from him."

"So you decided that you were the person to make the decision for me. That you somehow know better than I do what's right for my life." Although Caleb spoke quietly, the anger in his voice was unmistakable.

She shook her head. "I know it looks bad but that's not what happened. I was just trying to keep you from getting hurt."

"No. You put yourself in charge of deciding what was good for me and what wasn't."

"That's not true."

Caleb leaned over so that their faces were mere inches apart. She easily read the anger in his eyes. "The truth is you didn't respect me enough to tell me what your mother said. You didn't think I was strong enough to handle it."

"I didn't know who he was."

"*You* might not have known, but *I* had an idea that it was Brooks Langtree."

"You never said anything." Despite knowing she didn't have a right to know, Faith was still hurt by how little she mattered to him. They might be sleeping together, but that didn't make her special to him. Her feelings might be growing, but not his. It was safe to say he no longer felt the same affection he had before.

"I know you didn't just say that to me. Not after the secret you've been keeping. This is *my* search. My life. I don't owe you any information. I don't have to bare my soul to you. Given the fact that you've just proven yourself to be untrustworthy, I'm glad that I didn't tell you more. In fact, I regret sharing what I did."

"Really? Because if not for me, Hattie wouldn't know a thing about you. Nor would she be using her relationship with Brooks Langtree to set up a meeting between the two of you."

"Great. Thanks." His voice was anything but grateful and Faith knew that she and Caleb were veering close to a place where they would say things they would each regret. Words that they wouldn't be able to take back when their tempers cooled. That might not matter to Caleb now since he was positively furious with her, but it mattered to her. She was falling in love with him.

"I should go," she said softly.

"Yes, you should."

That harsh answer was painful, but she knew she'd earned his wrath. If she could go back and do it over, she would do it differently. She wouldn't keep anything from him. Better yet, she'd mind her own business.

She grabbed her purse and draped the strap over her shoulder. The hope that Caleb would say something to her dimmed as she crossed the small room. When she reached the door, she turned the knob and looked back at him. "I really am sorry, Caleb."

He only stared at her, his eyes icy. Realizing that she wasn't going to get an answer, she opened the door and left.

She trudged down the stairs and found Hattie sitting on the sofa in the main room. She stood when Faith entered.

"I didn't expect you to be here," Faith said.

"I figured you could use a friend." Hattie looped her arm with Faith's and they walked outside together.

"How did you guess?"

"Things were going pretty poorly between you and Caleb. I had a feeling they were only going to get worse."

"You were right. They did. He's furious with me."

"Do you blame him?"

Faith forced herself to admit the truth. "No. At the time I thought I was doing the right thing. Now that things have blown up in my face I realize that I should have handled it differently."

"So should your mother. I'm really disappointed in her."

"I tried to convince Mom to tell me the name, but she wouldn't. She was so sure that she was protecting Caleb from getting hurt."

"Like mother, like daughter I suppose." Hattie nudged Faith's shoulder affectionately. "Do you want to go to the diner and have an early lunch? It might make you feel better."

Faith nodded. "I really don't want to be alone. Caleb and I had plans for the day. Now I'm wondering if he'll ever forgive me."

"Of course he will. Now get in your car and follow me. I'm in the mood for a good salad."

As Faith drove to the Gemstone Diner, she tried to keep her mind from straying to Caleb and the disaster that their relationship had become. Hattie was getting out of her sedan when Faith arrived and they walked inside without speaking. After they'd placed their orders, Hattie looked directly at Faith. "Tell me what you plan to do next."

That was a surprise. She'd expected a lecture or some other form of recrimination. "Nothing. It was my 'doing something' that created this mess. Maybe I should just bow out and let Caleb take the lead."

"I wasn't suggesting that you try to run things. You're a Hawkins. It's not easy for us to sit back and let things happen, even if that is what the situation calls for."

"Is this one of those situations?"

"Yes. Give Caleb space for now. He needs it. I'm sure

his emotions are all over the place. That might account for the intensity of his anger. Be there to support him if he needs it."

"I can do that." Faith toyed with her French fry. "Do you really think he'll forgive me? Or do you think this is the end? Tell me the truth. I can handle it."

"I saw the way that man looked at you. Your relationship is far from over."

Faith blew out a relieved breath. "I hope you're right."

Hattie smiled. "When am I wrong?"

"Well, I can safely say not once in my lifetime."

"Right. Now let's eat and talk about something else. Unpleasant conversation is bad for digestion."

"Done."

The impromptu meal with Hattie was just what Faith needed.

They'd just finished eating their desserts when Hattie's phone rang. She answered and then smiled. "Thanks for calling me back, Brooks. I was hoping that we could meet."

Faith's heart sped up at the mention of Brooks's name. She tried to make sense of the conversation when she could only hear one side. She didn't want to get too excited but it sounded as if Hattie and Brooks were scheduling an appointment.

"I'll see you then," Hattie said and then ended the call.

"I take it that you're going to meet with Brooks Langtree."

Hattie nodded. "In half an hour. Without Caleb."

Faith grabbed the bill, perused it and then tossed money on the table to cover it as well as a generous tip. "I'm going with you."

"Are you asking me or telling me?"

"Whichever works best."

Hattie raised her eyebrows. "What if neither does?"

"I'll follow you." When Hattie only stared, Faith knew that tactic wouldn't work. She folded her hands and tried again. "Please let me go. Please."

"Are you the same woman who just said you were going to step back?"

"Yes. And I meant it. I'll tell Caleb about this meeting. That is if he ever talks to me again."

"Why do you want to go?"

"I have to see for myself that Brooks Langtree is a good man. My mother says that he didn't treat Caleb's birth mother very well. She really doesn't like him but you seem to. Or at least you don't dislike him."

"I didn't know his wife, but from what I gather, she and your mother were friends. Naturally Suzie holds a grudge against him."

"I guess I understand that. But I still want to look into his eyes. Hear his voice. That way I'll feel more comfortable about the situation."

"And if you don't like him? Then what? Are you going to try to keep him and Caleb apart?"

"No way. I've learned my lesson."

Hattie nodded.

"So I can come?"

"Yes." Hattie stood and held out her arm, ushering Faith out of the diner. "We got lucky. He's in town to shoot a commercial for Taylor Beef. We're meeting at his hotel room."

Faith's heart thudded as she drove to the Heights Hotel. By the time she parked behind Hattie's car and got out, it was racing. She could possibly be meeting Caleb's birth father. She really hoped that he was a good man.

Hattie took one look at Faith and patted her hand. "Calm down. You look like you're about to keel over."

Faith inhaled deeply and then blew out the breath. "I just really want him to be everything that Caleb hopes he is."

"Let's go inside so you can find out."

Faith and Hattie walked into the hotel. Hattie gave Brooks Langtree's name to the front desk clerk. The smiling woman called Brooks's hotel room before she gave them the room number. Faith crossed her fingers as they rode the elevator to the second floor.

Hattie knocked on the appropriately numbered door and it immediately swung open to reveal a smiling Brooks Langtree. He looked so much like Caleb it made Faith's heart ache.

"Hattie. I was so pleased to get your call. Come on in."

"Thank you." Hattie stepped inside and Faith followed. "I brought Faith with me. I hope that's okay."

"Of course it is." Brooks gave Faith a warm smile. "Welcome. I hope you had a nice birthday."

Faith returned his smile. "I did. Thank you."

Brooks had a suite and he led them to the comfortable seating area. "Can I get you something to drink? A soda? Water?"

"I wouldn't mind some water," Hattie said, sitting on the silver-and-black striped love seat.

"And you, Faith?" Brooks asked.

She really wanted to get to the reason they were here, but it would be rude to say that. She sat beside Hattie and folded her hands in her lap. "I'll take a water too, please."

"Three waters coming up," Brooks said, heading for the mini fridge. He handed Hattie and Faith bottles of water, keeping one for himself. He sat in the chair across from them, a smile on his face. "To what do I owe this pleasure?"

"I'm not usually at a loss for words," Hattie said, "but suddenly I'm not sure how to start."

"That sounds ominous," Brooks said, stiffening.

She shook her head and replied quickly. "It's nothing bad. At least not to me."

Brooks leaned back in his chair, and blew out a breath. "In that case, take your time. I don't have any plans for the next few hours."

Faith was impressed by the older man's calm demeanor and the patient way he treated her grandmother. That raised her estimation of him. In the quiet, Faith took the opportunity to study Brooks. She couldn't get over how much he looked like Caleb. Or rather, it was more accurate to say that Caleb resembled Brooks. They both had rich deep brown skin, carved cheekbones, deep brown eyes and an identical smile. They also had similar builds. Both were each about six feet tall with broad shoulders. They even had similar mannerisms. No wonder Faith had felt like she'd seen Caleb before.

"Well, I suppose I should just get to it," Hattie said at last.

Brooks nodded. "Whenever you're ready."

"I recently met a young man who believes he might be your son. If I'm wrong and I've offended you, I apologize."

Brooks's face lost color and his hands began to tremble. The bottle began to slip from his fingers and Faith jumped up and grabbed it before it hit the floor. Tears began running down Brooks's face, but he didn't seem to notice. "You know my boy? You know Caleb?"

Faith was shocked that Brooks knew Caleb's name. That emotion was quickly followed by relief that Brooks admitted to being Caleb's birth father.

"Yes," Hattie said. "I do. He's been trying to meet with you for a while now."

"So that's who it was." Brooks nodded, then explained, "My agent mentioned talking to a young man one day, but it never occurred to me that it could be Caleb."

"It was," Hattie said gently.

Brooks shook his head and spoke in a soft voice as if to himself. "I feel like I'm dreaming. I've been waiting for this day for the longest time. Practically from the moment I placed him in the social worker's arms and forced myself to walk away."

"I don't understand," Faith said. "You chose to give him up for adoption."

Brooks didn't take offense at her words or her accusatory tone. "I did."

"Why?"

"Faith. That's none of your business," Hattie admonished, sending her a look.

"It's okay. I don't mind answering," Brooks said. He turned his gaze to Faith. His eyes were turbulent with emotion. "I was so young when he was born. Only twenty. But I loved him from the first time I laid eyes on him. And I loved his mother. The three of us were a happy little family. But the rodeo promoter convinced us—or rather convinced *me*—to keep our marriage a secret. I was a rising star. They thought it would hurt my career if the public knew I had a wife and a child at my age. They liked the idea of a playboy bachelor image." His mouth twisted in obvious disgust. When he spoke again, his voice was filled with remorse. "It sounds so ridiculous now. I never should have agreed to it."

"You're looking at it with the wisdom of a fifty-year-old instead of the inexperience of a twenty-year-old," Hattie said gently.

"Even back then I had my doubts. But I also had a family to support, so I went along with it. So did Genie. And then Genie went back to work. I should have protested. It was only a few months after Caleb was born. But she said she was ready and that she missed competing. So I agreed." His sigh was filled with remembered pain. "One freak accident and Genie was gone. Suddenly I was a single father. Caleb was only a few months old. Barely able to hold up his head. He needed so much and I wasn't sure I could give it to him. I was broken, grieving the loss of the woman I loved."

Faith heard the agony in his voice and she experienced a rush of sympathy. He'd really been in an impossible situation.

"The only way I could support him was in the rodeo. But I couldn't care for him alone on the road.

"Then the social workers started coming around, telling me that it would be best for Caleb if I put him up for adoption. Genie and I didn't have any other family. All we'd had was each other. I might have made a different decision if I'd had someone else to turn to. But I didn't. Sure, there were my rodeo friends, but they were traveling just as much as I was. And what Caleb needed was stability. A home. A mother and a father. The social worker promised that he would be placed with a good family who would love him. From what I can see, they kept their word."

"How do you know that?" Faith asked.

"I've kept tabs on him from a distance. Although I couldn't be a part of his life, I needed to be sure that he was happy. That he was cherished."

"Why didn't you ever contact him? It's been thirty years." Faith knew that she didn't have a right to ask that question, but she couldn't help from advocating on Caleb's behalf. She was going to tell him about this meeting and she wanted to provide him with as much useful information as she could.

"It wasn't my place. I had no right to interfere in his life. When he was a kid, I didn't want to confuse him. I didn't know whether or not the Stroms had told him that he was adopted. If they hadn't I didn't want to be the one to break the news to him. Who knows what kind of harm that would have caused? It could have hurt Caleb and his relationship with his parents. I didn't want to do that." Brooks paused and blew out a long breath. "He had a father and it wasn't me. I didn't want Caleb to have to split his loyalties between the man who'd helped to create him and the man who'd raised him. That would have been a horrible thing to do to a child."

Brooks's voice grew low. If possible, he sounded even sadder. "Besides, I always thought he was better off without me. I was a rodeo rider, spending months at a time on the road, scratching out a living. A couple of days in this town, a couple days more in another. His adoptive father owned a successful business. He was at home every night for dinner with his family."

He looked at Faith, as if waiting for her next question. But she could only nod and wait for him to continue at his own pace.

"Then there was the question that I couldn't answer. Would Caleb even want to know me? Would he want me to be a part of his life? I didn't know, so I decided to let things be. If Caleb and I were ever meant to meet, it would happen on his terms and without interference from me."

"He has been searching for you for a few months," Faith said, quietly. "He wants to meet you."

"I want to meet him too." Brooks's voice quivered with emotion and more tears filled his eyes. Faith was elated as she realized that Brooks and Caleb wanted the same thing.

They wanted to meet.

"I'll call Caleb today. If it's okay with you, I'll give him your number," Faith said. She'd overstepped before and had learned her lesson. She was going to check with both parties before she made a move.

"That would be great," Brooks said, his smile bright despite the tears that stained his cheeks.

It was clear that the older man was overcome with emotion, so Hattie and Faith stood. Hattie said, "We're going to leave now, so you can have time to yourself. I know this has been a lot to absorb."

Brooks nodded absently. It was as if he were already imagining the reunion with his son. Then he shook off his stupor and jumped to his feet. He shook Hattie's hand effusively. "I'll never be able to thank you enough for what you've done for me and Caleb."

"You're quite welcome," Hattie said before she and Faith left.

Once they were alone in the hall, Faith turned to Hattie. "I have to tell Caleb about this. Or do you want to?"

Hattie laughed. "You know as well as I do that you want an excuse to call Caleb. This good news is the best reason of all. You should deliver it alone."

"You know me so well." Faith gave her grandmother a big hug. "I'll call him as soon as I get home."

"Good luck." Hattie said.

"Thanks. I'm going to need it."

On the drive home, Faith rehearsed what she planned to say. The second she stepped inside her house, she whipped out her phone and called Caleb. Her heart began to pound with tension as the phone rang. When she heard Caleb's voice, her practiced speech flew out of her head.

"This is Faith," she said.

"What can I do for you?" Caleb's voice was devoid of any emotion and her heart sank lower than she thought possible.

"Hattie and I met with Brooks Langtree just now. She told him about you and he wants to meet you. I told him that I would give you his telephone number. I hope that's all right."

Caleb didn't reply and Faith wondered if she'd overstepped again. As the silence stretched, her fear that he was never going to forgive her grew. Perhaps it really was over between them.

Chapter Thirteen

Caleb heard Faith's words, but he wasn't sure he actually heard them correctly. *Brooks Langtree wanted to meet with him?* The words echoed in his mind for a few moments before he was able to speak. "Say that again."

"Brooks Langtree is your father." Faith's voice was filled with glee.

"Did he say that?" Caleb asked cautiously and his back stiffened. The entire turn of events was shocking. Thirty years ago, the man had insisted that Caleb be given no information about him. And today he'd just told Hattie and Faith that he was Caleb's father. That was unbelievable.

Caleb's knees weakened. Suddenly woozy, he stumbled across the room and fell into a chair.

"Yes. I have his number if you want to talk to him."

Of course he wanted to talk to him. That was the entire reason he'd come to Bronco initially. Though he was elated beyond belief, his heart still ached from Faith's deception. Just thinking about how she'd withheld vital information from him still hurt. Secrets had kept him from his biological father for thirty years. The social workers and adoption agency had known the identity of Caleb's father, but hadn't shared it with him no matter how many times he'd asked. Faith had done the same thing.

She'd claimed that she'd been trying to protect him. He hadn't needed her protection. He'd needed her honesty. "What is the number?"

Faith gasped audibly and Caleb knew she'd been hurt by his abrupt response. He searched inside himself for some compassion for her, but he couldn't find any. His feelings were too raw at this time. Maybe later, he might be able to extend her some grace, but not now.

"Of course. I'll text it to you when we finish talking."

"Is there something more you need to say? Is this a power move on your part? Withholding the number until I've listened to you?"

"Of course not. I only wanted to apologize again. But clearly you don't want to hear it."

"You're right. There's nothing you can say to me right now. The only thing I want from you is Brooks Langtree's telephone number."

Faith didn't reply and he realized that she'd ended the call. He frowned but he had to admit that she'd only done what he'd requested. The phone beeped as a message came through.

His hand shook as he read the number. *His father's telephone number.*

Beads of sweat broke out on Caleb's forehead and he wiped his brow. His nerves jangled and he inhaled deeply and blew out the breath, trying to calm himself. His hand was trembling so much it took three attempts before he successfully tapped in the number. As the phone began to ring, Caleb's heart was pounding. And then a firm voice said hello.

"Brooks?" Caleb said, suddenly at a loss for words. He closed his eyes and started again. "This is Caleb Strom. I, uh… Hattie and Faith Hawkins spoke with you about me today. I…uh… I'm…"

"I know who you are, Caleb. You're my son." There was a long pause. Then Brooks continued in a shaky voice. "I've been waiting to talk to you for thirty years."

Brooks's emotional words dissolved Caleb's fear. Brooks—his father—had missed him. He hadn't turned his back on Caleb as he had often feared. There had been another reason. Now Caleb would finally learn the truth from the man himself. Caleb's vision blurred and he wiped away unshed tears. He hadn't expected to cry, but suddenly he couldn't stop the tears from falling. Before he knew it, big sobs were wracking his body.

"It's okay, son. I'm here." Brooks's voice broke and Caleb knew the older man was crying too.

Caleb took several deep breaths. Finally he regained sufficient control of himself to talk. He supposed he should give Brooks a quick summary of his life up to this point. Instead, he blurted out, "Why did you give me away? Didn't you love me? Didn't you want me?"

"Oh, Caleb," Brooks said and then sighed.

"Forget I said anything," Caleb said quickly. He didn't want to offend Brooks and get the conversation off on the wrong foot. Brooks might decide getting to know Caleb wasn't worth the recrimination. What was the point in bringing up a past they couldn't change? What mattered was the present. And possibly the future.

"No, son. I don't want to forget it. You have every right to ask that question. Ask me anything you want to know. Anything. Nothing is off-limits."

"Okay."

"And to answer your questions, I loved you with every fiber of my being. You and your mother were my world. After Genie died I wasn't in any position to take care of a baby. So I gave you to a loving couple who could give you what you needed."

"Did you ever regret giving me up?"

Brooks sighed. "Regret doesn't begin to describe my feelings. I wished there could have been another way. But there wasn't one. So I had to let you go."

"What was she like?"

"Your mother? I'm sorry. Is it okay to refer to Genie that way?"

"It's okay. So…her name was Genie?"

"Yes. Regina actually, but everyone called her Genie."

"Regina." Caleb tried the name on for size. He liked the way it sounded. "What was she like?"

"Genie was a tiny little thing, but she had the heart of a giant. She was gutsy and bold. Perhaps too bold for her own good. And ours."

"What do you mean?"

"Genie and I were still in our teens when we got together. We would have told the whole world about our marriage, but the rodeo managers advised us to keep it a secret. Very few people even knew about the baby—I mean you—and us."

More secrets.

"But it didn't make a difference to us. We were happy living in our private little world."

Caleb smiled at the picture that Brooks painted. It sounded so perfect. If Genie hadn't died, he might have spent his formative years on the rodeo circuit. He might have become a rider himself. It's possible that he could have met Faith years ago. Just thinking of her was painful and he shoved the thought aside.

"Genie was one of the best woman competitors on the tour. She didn't compete much when she was pregnant, so she was itching to get back into the ring. She started competing again when you were only a few months old. I shouldn't have let her."

"Why?"

"Because she was killed in a freak barrel racing accident. Her horse tripped. When they fell, the horse landed on her."

"I'm sorry to hear that." It sounded so cold and impersonal, especially since he was talking about his own mother.

"I know I have no right to ask this," Brooks said hesitantly, "but is it possible to meet in person?"

Caleb's heart leaped with hope. "When?"

"Anytime. Now if you can. I'm actually in Bronco. I can come to where you are. Or you can come here. I'm staying at the Heights Hotel in Bronco Heights. Whatever works best for you."

Caleb would lose it if he had to sit in this room, counting the minutes until Brooks arrived. He needed to do something. Driving to Brooks's hotel was preferable to waiting. "I'll come to you. I can be there in a few minutes."

"I look forward to seeing you soon."

After saying goodbye, Caleb grabbed his keys, raced from the room, jogged down the stairs and hopped into his truck. Before he turned on the ignition, he took several calming breaths, trying to slow his racing heart and quiet his mind. He didn't want to get into an accident.

When Caleb was sure he could drive carefully, he turned on the truck and started down the road. His mind was a jumble of thoughts and his emotions were scrambled. He forced himself to concentrate on his driving and tune out everything else.

Caleb reached the hotel and parked in the first spot he saw and then hurried into the lobby. He'd forgotten to ask Brooks for his room number, so he had to wait for the desk clerk to call Brooks for permission to give Caleb the room number. With the information in hand, Caleb climbed the stairs, two at a time. When he reached Brooks's floor, he stepped into the corridor and looked around, trying to get his bearings before heading down the hall.

Before he had taken two steps a door opened and Brooks Langtree stepped into the hall. Caleb stopped. Time froze as the men stared at each other. Then before he knew what was happening, Caleb found himself moving down the hall. At first he was walking. Then he was jogging. Running. Brooks must have been running too because they met in the middle. Brooks held out his arms. Without thinking, Caleb fell into the outstretched arms and felt Brooks's arms wrap around him. The embrace was strong and Caleb struggled to contain his emotions. He couldn't. Once more his body was shaking with sobs.

Eventually he became aware that Brooks was rubbing his back and murmuring soothing words to him. "I'm here, Caleb. I'm here."

Caleb sniffed and then pulled away, dragging his

sleeve over his wet face. He waited for embarrassment to swamp him, but the feeling never came. Brooks was wiping his own eyes and Caleb knew he had been just as affected by the meeting.

"Come on into my room," Brooks said, extending his arm.

"Thanks."

Once they were inside the hotel room with the door closed behind them, Brooks stared into Caleb's face. Slowly he smiled. "You look just like your mother."

"I was thinking that I look like you." Caleb took a breath. "Do you have a picture of her?"

"Just one with me." Brooks took a wallet out of his pocket, reached inside, pulled out a faded photograph and handed it to Caleb. He gave Caleb a crooked grin. "You're actually in this picture too."

Caleb eagerly looked at the tattered photo. There was an indentation from the wallet and he wondered how often Brooks had pulled it out over the years to look at. Though Brooks was also in the picture, Caleb's eyes instantly zeroed in on the woman's sweet face. Brooks had said they'd only been twenty when he'd been born, but that fact hadn't really sunk in. Now looking at his mother's image, he realized that she'd been barely out of her teens when he was born. As had Brooks. A decade younger than Caleb was now.

Although he'd tried to understand what Brooks had been telling him when he'd talked about that time in his life, Caleb had held onto a sliver of resentment at his father for giving him away. A part of him believed he should have tried harder to hold onto him. Now, seeing them smiling at the camera while Genie held a baby—

him—in her arms, he finally got it. They had been young. Too young.

Genie was radiant with joy that could only come from loving and being loved. The contentment on her face couldn't be faked. Caleb studied her face, looking for features they shared. He spotted some right way, although hers were more feminine. Delicate. Ever so slowly, he dragged his finger over the lines of her face, trying to connect with her. The picture was cool beneath his hand as expected, filling him with a deep sorrow. He wanted to know more about her.

"She was so happy to be your mother," Brooks said. "This may seem hard to understand, but she loved you a lifetime in the few months that she was blessed to be with you. I just wish you could remember that time."

So did Caleb. He would give anything to have a memory of sleeping in his mother's arms. He wished he could recall the sound of her voice or the smell of her skin. *Anything.* "Are there any videos of us together?"

"No. We didn't have a lot of money back then for things like that. People may have cameras on phones now, but they weren't as prevalent thirty years ago."

"I should have known that."

"I have a few more pictures. I can make copies for you if you want."

Caleb nodded. "That would be great."

They sat down and Brooks poured them drinks that neither of them touched. Brooks sighed and then glanced at Caleb with sorrow-filled eyes. "I felt guilty about her death for a long time. If she hadn't been in the ring that day she would still be alive today."

"I don't know much about rodeo, but I know that accidents happen and that they aren't anybody's fault," Caleb said.

"Taking care of a newborn is a lot of work. I knew she wasn't getting enough sleep and that she was worn out. But she insisted on competing. And I let her. Then she was gone. The pain in my heart was unbearable. Every time I looked into your beautiful face, I saw hers. I truly believed that giving you up was my punishment. After what I let happen to Genie, I didn't think I deserved to be your father. Not when she wasn't around to be your mother."

"That's not true. You didn't deserve to be punished. And neither did I."

Brooks gasped. "Please don't tell me that your parents weren't as kind to you as I have been led to believe."

Caleb shook his head. "No. My parents were great. Are great. They love me as much as any two people ever loved a child. But I deserved to know where I came from. I deserved to know about my biological parents. And since my birth mother was dead, you were the only person alive who could tell me. And you made it all but impossible for me to find you."

"You're right. I know a lot of time has passed, but I can tell you all about her now."

"And about you. The only things I know are what's available in the public record and that's limited to your career."

"That's pretty much out of habit. It was drilled into me as a young man to keep my private life private. I suppose I got used to keeping secrets."

"Are you married? Do you have other kids?" Caleb

felt a strange ache in his chest as he awaited Brooks's answer.

Brooks smiled. "Yes. And I want you to meet them. That is if you want."

"I would like to." The idea that there were more people in the world who were genetically related to him was mind-blowing. He knew that shared love could create a family of people who didn't share genes. Iris and Nathan Strom were his parents. They were a family. Nothing would ever change that. But still he liked knowing that there were more people in the world who were related to him. More family.

"Then I'll tell them about you and set up a meeting."

"How do you think they'll react? If learning about me will upset them, you don't have to do it. I don't want to cause any problems for you."

Brooks shook his head. "There won't be a problem. My wife knows that I was married when I was a teenager."

"Does she know about me?" Caleb held his breath, trying to ignore the dread creeping down his spine.

"Of course. You weren't a dirty little secret. You were my son."

Caleb breathed out a sigh of relief. "And your kids?"

"I have a son and two daughters. I can guarantee that they will be pleased to discover that they have an older brother. Especially my son, who has been outnumbered by his sisters."

The thought made Caleb smile. Over the years, many of his friends had told him about battles of the sexes in their own homes. As an only child, he'd listened to their complaints with a bit of envy. Now he knew that he actually did have siblings.

"How old are they?"

"Isabel is nineteen, Angelique is seventeen, and Craig is sixteen."

Caleb nodded. They were younger than he'd expected. But then, Brooks probably hadn't wanted to have kids as a young man again.

"It took me a while to get my head on straight after losing your mother and then you," Brooks said as if he'd read Caleb's mind. "I was numb for years. I didn't think that I deserved to be loved. I closed off my heart, unwilling to risk the pain. Rodeo became my life and I gave it my all. When I wasn't competing, I was traveling or practicing. That's it. That was my entire life for years."

"Did you win a lot?"

"I won just about everything. But having a great career didn't bring me even a bit of joy. I didn't come back to Bronco. Bronco was where I'd lost everything that mattered to me and being here hurt way too much."

Caleb nodded in understanding. He wouldn't want to visit the place where he'd lost his entire family either.

Brooks smiled. "Then I met Judith."

"Is she in rodeo, too?"

Brooks shook his head. "No. She's a tax accountant. We met at the movies and were friends for a long time. She helped me to forgive myself. It took a while, but she finally convinced me that there was nothing I could have done to prevent your mother's accident. After a while, I started to believe that I had the right to have a life again. A life that included love. The next thing I knew, we were dating. Then we fell in love. There's not much more to say about that."

Caleb could use his imagination to fill in the rest. Although he was only getting to know Faith, he could picture how it would feel to fall in love with her. That thought shocked him. He wasn't going to fall in love with Faith. They'd agreed that their relationship was going to be casual. Strictly physical. She'd been clear that she wasn't looking for romance. Neither was he.

He'd been trying to find his birth father and didn't have time for anything else. But now he had met Brooks and the search was over. His situation was different. Of course that didn't mean Faith had changed her mind.

Not that it mattered. He wasn't sure she was actually the type of woman she'd led him to believe she was. She'd kept secrets from him. He might forgive her for that one day. But today wasn't that day.

Brooks and Caleb talked a while longer, unwilling to part company. Then Brooks received a business call.

"I should go," Caleb said, pushing to his feet.

"Call me when you get back to the B and B so we can set up a time for you to meet everyone."

"I will," Caleb promised. He was walking on air as he strode down the stairs and back to his car.

He'd finally met his father. He would give anything to share the moment with Faith. Too bad he couldn't.

Faith emptied the bucket of dirty water into the toilet, flushed it and then yanked off her rubber gloves. She squatted on her haunches and sighed. Although she'd never kept score, this had to be the worst week of her life. She had hoped to hear from Caleb by now, but with every passing day, hope had seeped out of her. His silence was an unmistakable sign of how badly she'd hurt him. Proof of just how angry he was at her. At least, she prayed that was all it was. Otherwise his silence might mean he'd actually cut her out of his life.

She shoved that heartbreaking thought aside. She'd spent several days and nights checking to make sure that her phone was working. As if a broken phone was the reason she hadn't heard from him. She'd tried to focus, but she couldn't keep Caleb off her mind. Whenever she found herself thinking about him, she made herself do something else. Anything else. After eating more ice cream and potato chips than she should have, Faith decided to turn to constructive activities. She now had the cleanest home in the city of Bronco, if not the entire state of Montana.

This morning Faith had decided that she wasn't going to keep thinking about Caleb. If their relationship was over, there was nothing she could do to change it. She certainly wasn't going to force herself into his life.

She was returning the mop and bucket to the broom closet when her doorbell rang. Her heart leaped as she thought that Caleb had finally come to see her. Faith glanced in the mirror hanging over her sofa, hoping that she didn't look like she'd just mopped the kitchen and bathroom floors. She was sorely disappointed. Her ratty T-shirt gaped away from her torso and her jeans were threadbare in spots. Her clothes were damp in places and she looked like Cinderella before her fairy godmother worked her magic. Pausing for a moment, she removed the scrunchie, ran her fingers through her hair and then redid her ponytail, looking slightly less bedraggled.

She turned away from the mirror. This was as good as it was going to get.

"Coming," she called as she rushed through the spotless front room. Inhaling deeply, she pulled open the door. And sagged. It wasn't Caleb. "Oh."

"Is that any way to greet your mother?" Suzie asked.

"Sorry." Faith forced a smile. "Come on in."

"Don't mind if I do." Suzie swept inside and paused. She inhaled. "Furniture polish. Window cleaner. Bleach. What's wrong?"

There was no sense in pretending. "Caleb and I had a falling-out."

"Oh no. I'm sorry to hear that. What happened?" Suzie sat on the sofa and then patted the seat beside her.

Sighing, Faith sat down. As she spoke, she struggled to keep her voice steady. "He was angry when he discovered that I had kept information about his birth father from him. I tried to explain that I didn't have any facts to share, but he wasn't hearing that. Hattie arranged a meeting with his father, but that didn't change things between us. We haven't talked in a week."

"Oh, Faith. I'm so sorry."

Faith shrugged. It would be easy to blame her mother for what happened—she'd withheld vital information from Faith—but Suzie really wasn't at fault. It had been Faith's choice to keep what little she'd known from Caleb. Besides, assigning blame wouldn't change things. "It's over now."

"I was trying to keep from hurting Caleb. Instead I ended up hurting you."

"You aren't the one who hurt me."

"Maybe not directly, but I put you in a position to

be hurt. If I'd either told you everything I knew or told you nothing, Caleb wouldn't have a reason to be upset with you."

"Maybe. But hindsight is twenty-twenty and all that. The main thing is that he has found his father. He and Brooks Langtree have been in contact." Faith turned to her mother. "Brooks is nothing like you said. He's a good man."

Suzie sniffed. "Time changes people. Sounds like it was for the better in his case."

Faith imagined that was as good as it was going to get. Suzie's loyalty to her late friend wouldn't allow for much else. "I guess. Anyway, it worked out for them. Everything else is secondary."

"You're saying what you think I expect you to say, which is nice but not necessary. You can be honest about your feelings with me. I won't judge you."

Faith blew out a breath. "I'm feeling hurt and left out. Caleb would never have gotten to meet with Brooks Langtree if not for Grandma. Grandma wouldn't have been involved if I hadn't asked for her help on his behalf."

"And you want his gratitude?"

"No." She wanted his love. "But I think he should at least give me the benefit of the doubt. He should have given me a chance to explain why I did what I did."

"Maybe given time he will."

"I've given him time. It's been a week. How much time does he need?"

"I don't have the answer to that question. But maybe you're spending too much time focusing on him and not enough time focusing on your own life."

"What do you mean? I'm taking care of my life. I've been working hard on my career. I've also been taking care of my home. You can't possibly think that I'm neglecting anything."

"This place is spotless. Evidence that you're trying to keep yourself busy so you don't have to face your feelings. That in and of itself is a sign that you need to get yourself together."

"Meaning?"

"You've been spending a lot of your time and energy helping Caleb."

"He's my friend."

"And more?"

There had never been a good time to lie to her mother. Suzie was much too astute to be fooled. Besides, apart from a few rough years when Faith had been an angsty teen who hadn't been on good terms with most people, she and her mother had always shared a close relationship. Suzie would understand how she felt.

Faith sighed. "I was beginning to consider the possibility."

"I had a feeling," Suzie said slowly. She smiled and then it faded. "But he has so much going on in his life at the moment. I can only imagine the number of emotions he's feeling right now. He probably can't even tell you how he feels because he might not know."

"This has been a very emotional time for him. But he'd managed to compartmentalize before and we had a great time together."

"I don't doubt that. But now that he and Brooks have met, Caleb will be dealing with a lot more emotions. They'll probably be spending time getting to know each other. That is, if Brooks is interested in getting to know Caleb," Suzie scoffed.

"I met Brooks. He was so happy to learn that Caleb had been looking for him. He was eager to meet Caleb in person. I have no doubt that they'll be spending more time together in the future."

"With all that going on, he probably doesn't have a lot of time for a relationship," Suzie said.

"What are you saying?"

"Maybe it's best if you step back too. Stop spending so much time trying to avoid your feelings or waiting to hear from Caleb. Get back to living your life."

"I'm trying."

"I know. Of course, if you run out of things to do around here, you can always come over to my house. I've been trying to get your dad to paint the kitchen for weeks, but he hasn't picked up a roller yet. You can always take over that task. There certainly isn't any more cleaning to do around here."

Faith laughed. "I'll consider the offer."

"You do that." Suzie rose. "I need to get going. I just wanted to make sure that you're okay. I'll see you later."

Faith hugged her mother and then watched as Suzie got into her car and drove away. Though she didn't want to admit it, her mother was right.

It was time to let Caleb go and move on with her life.

Chapter Fourteen

"So, tell us everything. We want to hear everything from the beginning," Iris said, settling on the sofa beside Nathan. Caleb sat in a chair across from his parents. He'd called his parents right after he'd met with Brooks, but he'd been so emotional that he couldn't express himself correctly. He and Brooks had spent time together every day this past week, eating dinner or just sitting and talking so they could get to know each other better. Though his parents had been overjoyed for him, and would have understood if he'd stayed in Bronco even longer, he'd made it a point to be here for Sunday dinner.

"It's been good. And strange." Caleb leaned forward and clasped his hands together. After he and Brooks had gone their separate ways that first day, Caleb had been too amped up to sit still. He couldn't call Faith and discuss his feelings. He was still upset with her and was unsure how the conversation would go. Their last one had been pretty bad. So he'd called his parents. They'd deserved to know that he had met his birth father.

"Strange? You're going to have to explain that answer a bit," Nathan said.

Caleb nodded, took a deep breath and then started over, recounting the entire story from beginning to end.

The first time he'd told them the story, he'd glossed over a lot of what Brooks had told him. Now he didn't leave out a single detail. Every once in a while, one of his parents would ask a question for clarification, but for the most part he was able to just tell the story without interruption. When he finally reached the end, he felt a little bit wrung out as if he'd relived that emotional moment. And relieved.

Iris took a sip of her coffee and then set the mug onto the coaster. "That explains a lot."

"It does?" Caleb asked. He wasn't exactly sure what his mother was referring to, but he had no doubt she would explain.

"Yes. After blaming himself for the tragic loss of his wife, and feeling unable and undeserving of raising you, I understand why he didn't want to make it easy for you to contact him."

"Now you've totally lost me," Caleb said, shaking his head. Did his very own mother agree that Brooks had been right to make it hard for Caleb to find him? "That is one thing that I still don't understand. If he loved me, but couldn't take care of me, it seems like he would have wanted to stay in touch. Or at least make it possible for me to find him."

"Imagine how horrible he would feel if you knew how to get in touch with him but you didn't reach out. By making it hard, he could always tell himself that you might want to meet him but were unable to. I know it doesn't make a lot of sense to you, but it was his way of protecting himself from further pain."

"I see your point even if I don't agree with his decision," Caleb said after a while.

"So, what's next?" Nathan asked.

"He wants me to meet his wife and kids. His wife knows about me, but his kids don't, so he's going to tell them about me this week."

"How do you feel about that?"

"I'm okay with meeting them if they want to meet me. When I went in search of my biological father, I didn't think about anything else. It never occurred to me that he might have a family that would want to meet me. I didn't want to get my hopes up too high."

Nathan nodded. "That's reasonable."

"So, you intend to keep in touch?" Iris asked.

"That depends," Caleb said slowly.

"On what?" Nathan asked.

"On how the two of you feel about it. You're my parents. You're the ones who have been here all my life. You're the ones I've always depended on. You supported me when I wanted to find my birth father, but that doesn't mean you want him or his family to become a part of my life. A part of *our* lives. Whatever happens between me and Brooks will affect all of us. If you don't want to deal with Brooks and his family, I can meet them once and then that can be the end of it."

"Don't even think that way," Iris said. "We love you too much to ever be that selfish."

"We always knew there would be a possibility that you would want to have a relationship with him," Nathan said, looking Caleb in the eyes. "And we're fine with it."

"Are you sure?"

"Positive," Iris added. "In fact, we're grateful to Brooks. If not for him, we wouldn't have had the chance to have such an amazing son. And you are our son. Brooks Langtree's presence in your life won't change that. Nor will it change our love for you. And we do love you."

Caleb's throat tightened and his vision blurred for a moment. He knew his parents loved him. They'd told him and shown him that his entire life. Their reaction now was only further proof of that. "Right back at you."

"So meet his family. Hopefully, you and your siblings will become close friends," Iris said. "And if they're amenable, we would like to meet all of them."

"Really?" Caleb asked. He didn't know why he was surprised. His parents were the most loving people he'd ever met. Naturally they would be welcoming to Brooks and his family.

"Of course. Invite them over for dinner," Iris said and Nathan nodded. "Of if they would prefer to meet in a restaurant, we can do that too."

"You two are the best," Caleb said. He stood and gave each of his parents a big hug.

"You aren't just noticing that, are you?" Nathan asked, grinning.

"No. But I don't tell you often enough how much I appreciate you."

"We know how you feel," Iris said. "We've always known."

"And speaking of girlfriends," Nathan said, ignoring the fact that they hadn't been talking about girlfriends at all, "how is Faith? I imagine she must be pretty happy about the turn of events."

Although Caleb had mentioned the role Faith had played in his search, he hadn't told his parents that she'd withheld information from him. For an unknown reason, he still felt the need to protect her.

Now he frowned. "We aren't together any longer."

"What happened?" Iris asked.

Caleb gave them the abridged version of Faith's actions, trying to keep her from sounding bad. Though she'd hurt and disappointed him, she wasn't a bad person. And she hadn't meant to hurt him. He saw that now.

"Wow," Nathan said, tapping his fingertips together. "So when do you intend to call her?"

"I don't," Caleb said flatly. "There have been so many secrets in my life. She knew how I felt about them, but she kept information from me anyway."

"Her heart was in the right place," Iris said. Naturally she would frame Faith's actions in the best possible light. Iris could find the good in anyone.

"That doesn't change anything. Mom, aren't you the one who always says that impact matters more than intent?"

"I am. But that doesn't mean intent doesn't matter. Especially when the action was done out of love. I haven't met Faith, but from everything you've told me, I have no doubt that she was only trying to protect you."

Those had been Faith's very words.

"You know that, don't you?" Nathan asked when Caleb didn't respond.

"Don't you, son?" Iris repeated.

Caleb looked at his parents. They had made their mistakes in the past. With him and with each other. That was the nature of relationships. Yet their love had always been enough to get them through the rough patches. Would love be enough to get him through this rough patch with Faith?

That thought came out of nowhere and it stunned him. But only for a moment. Suddenly it was abundantly clear how he felt about Faith. It made sense that he would always want to protect her. *He loved her.* Now he believed that she'd tried to protect him because she loved him, too. Was he going to let one well-meaning mistake cost him the love of a lifetime? No way. "I know."

"So, what are you going to do?" Iris asked.

"I'm going to go to Faith and straighten out this mess." There might be some groveling involved. In fact, he would bet on it. But he would gladly beg. He'd do whatever it took to get Faith back into his life where she belonged.

"That's my boy," Nathan said.

Faith stared blankly at the television. None of the characters looked familiar. The mystery she'd been pretending to watch had gone off and been replaced by a reality show, her least favorite form of entertainment. She grabbed the remote and then turned off the TV. Silence would be preferable.

She checked the time. It was eight o'clock. She supposed it was late enough for her to go to bed. Not that it mattered. She expected to toss and turn for hours as she'd done every night since she and Caleb had broken up. Hopefully, exhaustion wouldn't take long to claim her tonight.

Tossing aside the fleece throw that covered her lap, Faith stood and headed for the stairs. Before she had taken two steps, her doorbell rang. Her heart skipped a beat, but she immediately told herself to calm down. She wasn't going to play that game again. Over the past week, each time her doorbell had rung, she'd run to the door, hoping to find Caleb standing on the other side. Each time she'd been disappointed to see her mother, sisters or cousins. Once it had been a delivery guy with the wrong address. She didn't know who was ringing her bell now, but she knew it wasn't Caleb. They were done.

Not bothering to brush the potato chip crumbs from her old comfy sweatshirt or check her appearance in the mirror, she opened the front door. And gasped.

"Caleb. What are you doing here?"

He looked so good in his black leather jacket, red-and-black plaid shirt and faded jeans. One arm was behind his back. Though it was tempting to run a hand over her messy hair, she resisted the urge. Caleb already knew that she was flawed, so he wouldn't be surprised by her less than glamorous appearance. If he even cared what she looked like, which was doubtful.

"Can I come in?" he asked.

"Sure." She stepped aside. She'd given up hoping to ever see him again. Now hope tried to sprout in her heart, but she nipped it in the bud. This wasn't some romance novel where things always worked out. This was the real world where hearts got broken.

Before he entered, Caleb pulled his arm from behind his back. He was holding a dozen red roses. "These are for you."

"Why?" she asked, automatically taking the bouquet. She held them up to her nose and inhaled. They smelled so good. So sweet. That stubborn hope tried once more to spring up. This time she let it.

He stepped inside, closed the door, then led her into her front room. She took a peek at his eyes. The anger that had filled them the last time she'd seen them was gone. Now she saw doubt. "For a lot of reasons. First, I realize that I have never given you flowers. I'm ashamed of that fact now."

"Why? We weren't dating. Our relationship has always been strictly casual. I didn't have any expectations."

The corners of his mouth turned down as if her answer displeased him. "Faith..."

She didn't have the emotional fortitude to discuss their relationship. She was still trying to accept the fact that it was over. These guilt flowers weren't helping. "And the other reasons?"

He sighed as if disappointed. "To apologize to you."

"For what?" Faith asked.

"For being such a jerk." Caleb shook his head slowly. His voice was filled with remorse. "I was wrong to treat you the way that I did. I was upset, but that doesn't excuse my behavior. There was no reason to act like I did."

"I understand. Looking back, I could have done things differently too. I should have pressed my mother for more information. And even if she didn't tell me more, I should have let you know what she'd said. Perhaps she would have been willing to tell you more than she'd told me."

"You were trying to protect my feelings. You both were. I see that now."

"Yes. But you're an adult. A man. You didn't need protecting."

He reached out and took the bouquet from her hands and set it on the table. Then he took her hands into his. Their eyes met. His were filled with warmth and affection. "Everyone could use protection at one time or another. I know you were only trying to help me. It was a lot easier to lash out at you than to face my fear of being rejected by Brooks."

"I understand."

"So, can you forgive me for being a jerk?"

Her heart, which had been lifting at his words, now began to soar. "If you can forgive me for keeping a secret."

He smiled. "Let's start fresh now."

"That's a plan I can get behind." The sorrow that had been Faith's constant companion for the past week vanished and she sighed. Caleb bent down and Faith rose on her tiptoes. Their lips brushed in a gentle kiss that soothed all of her hurts and put their conflict behind them. She pulled back, then leaned her head against his chest. It felt so good to be in his arms again.

He gave her a lopsided grin. "You know, you have a way of seeing me. The real me. You know what I'm feeling even before I do."

"I wouldn't go that far."

"I would." He slid his arms from around her back and placed his hands on her waist. "Look into my eyes. Can you see what I feel?"

She met his gaze and her heart stuttered. His eyes were filled with an emotion she'd longed to see but hadn't dared to hope for. Instead of answering his question, she nibbled on her bottom lip. "I'm afraid to say it. I don't want to get things wrong again."

"Then I'll say it. I love you, Faith. I've been falling for you since the day we met. But there was so much going on in my life, I didn't notice. Plus I didn't think I had the emotional bandwidth to add anything else. Boy, was I wrong." He grinned briefly before letting it fade away. "That's not completely honest. The truth was I was afraid of putting my heart on the line. More afraid than I was of being rejected by my biological father."

"I was a bit wary myself," Faith confessed. "That's part of the reason I wanted to keep things casual between us. You can't get hurt if you don't put yourself out there." Or so she'd thought.

"Playing it safe doesn't work for me anymore."

"We don't have to rush things," Faith said. "I know you have a lot to deal with now. I love you, Caleb and I'm not going anywhere. We can take things slowly."

Caleb shook his head. "I don't want to go slow. This past week without you has been hell. I missed you more than I ever would have believed was possible. I don't want to spend more time away from you than I have to. I need you in my life. I realize now that I don't have to solve all of my problems on my own. That it's okay and even better to have a partner to walk beside you. A partner to help you through the troubled times."

She smiled. "I feel the same way."

"There's so much we don't know about each other and I don't want to get ahead of myself, Faith. But I think we should be each other's partners. What do you say?"

"I say, sign me up."

"I was hoping you'd say that." He lowered his head and kissed her again. This time the kiss was hot. Passionate. Everything she'd been missing and feared she'd never feel again.

She was unbuttoning his shirt when he covered her hand with his, stopping her progress. He pulled back abruptly. She opened her eyes and glanced at him.

"I would love to introduce you to my hometown. And to my parents. How do you feel about that?"

"I would love to see your hometown and to meet your parents."

He grinned. "I was hoping you would say that."

The following Sunday

Faith stood beside Caleb on the sidewalk in front of the rambling house where he'd grown up. Set on a slight hill, with concrete stairs leading up to the wide porch, this was exactly the kind of place she could imagine Caleb living in as a child. From the pots of mums on either side of the front door, to the neatly trimmed bushes that lined the front porch, everything about the house was welcoming. There was an enormous tree in the center of the lawn, the perfect place for a tire swing. This was more than a house where people lived. This was a home filled with love.

Faith suddenly felt nervous, fearful that Iris and Nathan Strom would find fault with her. She was wearing a red sweater, red plaid skirt and black tights. In place of her cowboy boots, she was wearing black pumps. Suddenly she wished she had worn something—anything—else.

It didn't make sense to be filled with such trepidation. She had spoken with Iris and Nathan a couple of times this past week. They'd been more than gracious to her. There was no reason to expect them to be less than warm today.

Caleb gave her a smile that let her know he understood how she felt. "My parents are going to love you."

Faith exhaled. "I hope so."

"I know so."

Before Faith could say another word, the front door swung open and a middle-aged couple stepped onto the porch and hurried down the stairs. Caleb introduced them and his mother pulled Faith into a warm embrace that soothed all of Faith's worries. After a moment, Iris pulled back, keeping an arm around Faith's waist. "It's chilly outside. Let's go inside where we can talk and get to know each other better."

Faith immediately felt at ease. She glanced at Caleb, who smiled and nodded at her. She hadn't been looking for love, but love had found her and she couldn't be happier.

Her future was looking better than ever.

* * * * *

Look for the next installment in the new continuity

Montana Mavericks: The Trail to Tenacity
The Maverick's Christmas Kiss
by JoAnna Sims

On sale November 2024
Wherever Harlequin books and ebooks are sold.

And don't miss the previous books,
Redeeming the Maverick
by New York Times *bestselling*
author Christine Rimmer

The Maverick Makes the Grade
by USA TODAY *bestselling*
author Stella Bagwell
Available now!